HER
DADDY'S
EYES

GARY E. PARKER

Revell
Grand Rapids, Michigan

© 2006 by Gary E. Parker

Published by Fleming H. Revell
a division of Baker Publishing Group
P.O. Box 6287, Grand Rapids, MI 49516-6287
www.revellbooks.com

Printed in the United States of America

Library of Congress Cataloging-in-Publication Data
Parker, Gary E.
    Her daddy's eyes / Gary E. Parker.
        p.   cm.
    ISBN 0-8007-3123-9
    1. Southern States—Fiction. I. Title.
PS3566.A6784H47 2006
813'.54—dc22   2005029217

SECTION 1

There's something greater
That speaks to the heart alone:
'Tis the voice of the great Creator
Dwells in that mighty tone.

Joseph Edwards Carpenter

1

Allie Wilson sat on the floor of her childhood bed-room in a pair of lightweight cotton pajamas. The tiny image of a blond-haired, green-finned mer-maid—repeated over and over again—decorated the pa-jamas. The hems of the legs and the cuffs on the sleeves were frayed, thinned by years of wear and tear. A light May breeze blew through an open window to her left. A ceiling fan whirred gently. An arrangement of freshly cut flowers sat in a crystal vase on a table by her head. A stack of books, picture frames, shoes, old baseball caps, and a cluster of other assorted items surrounded her on the floor. Allie heard footsteps and looked up as her mom, Gladys, entered the room.

"I like your pajamas," her mom said, pointing to Allie's frayed nightwear.

"You should. You gave them to me."

"Christmas—when you were thirteen."

Allie smiled as she remembered the Christmas tradition; her mom gave her new pajamas on Christmas Eve every year. Still did. "I always liked mermaids," she said.

Gladys plopped down beside her. "They're a bit snug in the backside now, I expect," she teased.

"And a little short in the legs but not too bad."

"You got most of your height that year," Gladys said. "Five ten by thirteen."

"I'm wearing them for old times' sake."

"I'm surprised you found them."

"They were stuck in the back of a dresser drawer. You know me. I never throw anything away."

"You're the queen of the pack rats."

Allie surveyed the clutter around her. "Until now," she said.

"You're finally cleaning things out?" Gladys's voice registered surprise.

Allie picked up a pair of high heels that had once been favorites but that she hadn't worn in years. "About time, don't you think?"

Her mom chuckled. "I guess a wedding in three weeks causes a girl to do all kinds of strange things."

Allie grinned at her mom. Gladys, now fifty-three, was stout but not plump, and age lines traced around her mouth and eyes, but more from laughing than anything else. She was gray haired but with no shame about it. "I earned every gray hair on me raising a daughter mostly by myself," she said whenever anybody asked her why she didn't buy a younger hair color from a bottle.

Allie held up the high heels. "You know anybody who can use these? I want to give away what I don't need anymore."

Gladys took the size nine and a half heels, her eyes bright. "You can search the neighborhood for a tall Cinderella, I guess," she said, "but no short girl can wear these skis."

Allie tossed a cushion at her mom, who caught it with one hand and placed it behind her back.

6

"I bought those heels, what . . . twelve years ago?" Allie asked, trying to remember.

"The year you graduated from Furman."

"I wore them the first game I ever coached; they made me taller than any of my players."

"I'm glad you were never ashamed of your height."

"You taught me not to slump."

"It's a good thing Trey is six three."

Allie thought of her fiancé, Trey Thompson—gangly, blue-eyed, and blond. He worked as a guidance counselor at Asheville High School, where she'd once taught and served as the assistant basketball coach. Although she'd since left that school for the head coaching job at Crestview High—a new school in her hometown of Harper Springs, North Carolina, a four red-light mountain town about thirty minutes west of Asheville—they still saw each other just about every day and had done so for the past three years. For over two years now, Trey had asked her to marry him on every special occasion that showed up on the calendar. Her birthday, Christmas, Valentine's Day, his birthday, Mother's Day. Once he'd even asked on St. Patrick's Day.

"It will make every guy I know green with envy," he'd said. "My marrying a woman who looks like a model, long and willowy, raven hair, eyes the color of black olives."

Until just recently she'd always told him to wait. "I'm not ready yet," she'd say. "You know why."

"Let me see," Trey would say, cupping his chin in an exaggerated counseling pose. "Could it be that your father's abandonment of you and your mother when you were just four has caused you to become distrustful of the entire male species?"

Allie always laughed but just barely. Although she'd never whined to Trey about the absence of a dad, he knew the story. "Just don't give up on me," she constantly pleaded.

"You'll find that I'm a stubborn man," he'd assure her. "Until you kick me away with a pointy-toed boot, I won't give up on you."

True to his word, Trey had kept asking, and finally, on Valentine's Day she'd said yes.

Her mom placed the high heels in a box, and Allie's mind returned to the present.

"You plan to leave anything here?" Gladys asked.

Allie stood, stepped to the window, and looked out at the yard of the white two-story house her mom's folks had given her when they passed on. A rope dangled from a tall oak directly ahead of her. A tire had once swayed on the end of the rope, and she'd spent hours on hot summer days swinging on the tire. When not on the tire, she'd spent another big chunk of her time shooting basketball on a goal attached to a pole just off the side of the house where her mom parked the car. A small porch ran down the side where the goal hung, and that porch and the town of Harper Springs, which lay three miles past it, gave her the third and fourth major reference points of her youth. On a lot of afternoons, she and her mom had sat on the porch to shuck corn or snap peas or cut the okra they grew in their garden out behind the house.

Allie's throat filled as she faced her mom again. Although she kept a small apartment a couple of blocks from the school, mostly to remind herself that she was a grown woman and shouldn't live with her mom anymore, most of her belongings remained right here in this room where she'd grown up. The notion of ridding herself of most of the junk of her youth, of cleaning out her belongings and walking away from this house forever, scared her more than any woman her age ought to admit. It wasn't that she didn't want to get married. Quite the contrary. Although Trey wasn't perfect, she'd stopped believing that any man was and so looked forward to settling down with him, perhaps even beginning a family. But actually clearing out everything she owned, everything she'd collected in her lifetime, seemed too sharp a cleavage with the past, like stepping off a cliff in the dark. Allie's eyes moistened slightly, but she brushed them clear, moved to the closet, and started hauling out a stack of boxes from the far corner.

Gladys took the boxes and stacked them on the floor. After removing all the boxes from the closet, Allie found a place on the floor by Gladys again. Her mom flipped the lid off the top box. A pair of white shoes sat inside.

"Give them to the Community Clothes Closet," Allie said.

Her mom dropped the box to the side and opened another. A bunch of pictures lay inside. Allie flipped quickly through the photos, most of them showing her in various states of shooting a basketball.

"I was a skinny thing," she said as she finished examining the box and shoved it to the side.

"Like a young filly," Gladys said. "Still are, though you're not such a young filly anymore."

"Hey, I'm just thirty-three!"

"Close to over-the-hill; in my day if a woman didn't marry by the time she turned thirty, she officially entered the ranks of the old maids."

9

"Heaven forbid that should happen." Allie flipped the top off another box. An old corsage, its flower long since dried, rested inside. Allie held it to her nose, took a breath, and imagined she could still smell the scent of the bloom.

"Tenth grade," she said, remembering the homecoming dance when she received the corsage.

"What was that boy's name?"

"Bill Stone. He moved away a couple of years later. Wonder what happened to him." She dropped the corsage back in the box.

"A keeper or a goner?" her mom asked, pointing to the corsage.

Allie hesitated but then waved it away. "Bill Stone is a goner," she said.

Her mom smiled. "You really are cleaning out, aren't you?"

Allie lifted another box and found more pictures in it, black and white ones this time. Her brow furrowed as she fingered the top photo—a picture of her grandmom and granddad standing in front of the house where she now sat.

"What are these?" she asked, handing the first picture to Gladys and reaching for the second.

Gladys's eyes widened as she examined the image. "I thought I'd lost these," she said.

Allie lifted out several more. They showed her in scenes she couldn't remember, younger than she recollected. "Have I ever seen these?" she asked, feeding them to Gladys.

Gladys took the pictures one by one. "I don't know," she said.

Allie thumbed through more pictures. Then her fingers froze as she stared at one in the middle of the stack. Two young couples, the men in military uniforms, the women in calf-length white dresses and gloves, laughed out at her from the print. A black Cadillac served as a prop for the happy couples. The women sat demurely on the hood, their legs hanging over the front. The men stood on either side of the women, their feet propped rakishly on the silver bumper of the Cadillac.

Allie immediately recognized her mom as one of the women and knew, without recognizing him, the identity of the man directly to her mom's left. Jack Wilson, long as a fence rail and equally thin, a dimple in his chin, black hair falling onto his forehead.

"It's Dad," she said softly.

Gladys leaned over, saw the picture, and grabbed for it and the box at the same time, but Allie held them away from her.

"Let me have those!" Gladys said.

Allie shook her head.

"They're just old pictures," her mom said, still reaching for the box. "No reason to drag them out now."

Allie pulled all the pictures from the box, dropped it to the floor, and stood. Her mom stood with her.

"Give me the pictures," Gladys insisted, her teeth clenched. "They're mine!"

"Why don't you want me to see them?" Allie asked, holding the pictures over her head like a grown-up holding something from a child.

Gladys shrugged. "It's just . . . there's no reason to drag out old memories, that's all."

Allie lowered the pictures and handed them to her mom. "I'd like to see them," she said, "but I'll do what you want."

Gladys held the photos for several seconds, then sighed and handed them back to Allie, who took the one of her dad and inspected it more closely.

"It's Jack just before he left for Vietnam," Gladys said.

"I've never seen this picture."

"You weren't born yet. I didn't even know I was pregnant at the time."

"You're pregnant in this?"

"Just barely. I was nineteen years old, your dad too."

Allie studied the image a few more seconds, then flipped to the next one. "So he's the same age as you."

"Yes."

"Hard to believe."

"You've never seen any of those," her mom said, nodding toward the rest of the prints in Allie's hands.

Allie thumbed through six more images, all of her mom and dad in various places and poses. In the third one, a little girl stood between her mom and dad, a little girl in a light-colored dress, a pair of black shoes with a buckle on them, and a bonnet on her head. Her eyes—bigger than seemed right for her small frame—bugged out, brightly shining toward the person taking the picture.

"It's me," Allie said.

Gladys stepped to her side and studied the picture. "Yes," she finally said.

"How old was I?"

"Three."

"The year before dad left us?"

"Yes."

"Do you have other pictures of me with dad?"

"Not many, perhaps a few."

"Can I see them?"

"Of course you can."

"Why haven't you shown them to me?"

Her mom shrugged. "Didn't want you to remember bad things, to conjure up the fact that Jack left us. You want to see them now?"

Allie thought a moment, then shook her head. "Another time maybe."

"Whenever you want."

Allie nodded, not doubting that her mom had done what she thought best for her. Although Gladys hadn't shut out all talk about her dad, she never brought it up either. In Allie's younger years, her mom had answered all the questions Allie had asked as best she could.

"Why did Dad leave us?" she'd asked often during the first couple of years after he left.

"He had some troubles," her mom always explained. "Brought them back from the war."

"What kind of troubles?"

"He never really told me."

"Where did he go when he left us?"

"I don't know. He writes every now and again. Would you like me to read the letters to you?"

Allie always said yes, and her mom hauled out all the letters and they sat down, usually with hot chocolate in the winter and sweet iced tea in the summer, and Gladys read the letters to her over and over until they were both exhausted.

After a few years, the letters stopped coming and her dad disappeared for good, and Allie stopped asking about him. The young are curious but not overly persistent, she realized now. They adjust to life as it is and feel that the reality of the moment is normal. That's what she'd done.

Allie focused again on the face of her father in the picture. His eyes stared at her as if looking past the years, through them, penetrating the time and space that separated father from child. A sharp sense of nostalgia rolled over her, not for what had been—for she'd never known her dad—but for what might have been, what she might have experienced.

"I wish he could be here for my wedding," Allie said softly.

Gladys eased closer and put a hand on her back, both of them intent on the image of Jack Wilson. "I wish he could have been here for a lot of things for you," Gladys said.

Allie turned to Gladys as her eyes filled. All the grief from all the years caused by not having a dad suddenly threatened to overwhelm her. Feelings she didn't know she possessed welled up and spilled over. "What happened to him, Mom?" she asked.

"I wish I knew more, but I don't. He came back from Vietnam a broken man. Suffered nightmares, sweats, the shakes, took to drinking, maybe some drugs too. I never knew all of it."

"Did he ever say what happened to him over there?"

"Not much. Just that it was rough." Her voice trailed off, and she fell silent.

Allie knew to ask no more. "Do you think he really loved us?" she asked.

Her mom hesitated for only an instant. "I know it's hard to believe since he left us, but I know he did. He used to tell me over and over again that we were the only things that kept him alive. He sent money to us for years after he left, even after he stopped writing. He loved us. I believe that even though I don't have a lot of ways to prove it."

Allie wiped her eyes and tried to figure it all out. If he loved them, then why leave, no matter how tormented? She examined the question from every angle she could imagine, and something odd occurred to her. She voiced it before understanding it. "Maybe he left us because he loved us," she suggested.

"How do you figure that?"

Allie weighed her words carefully but then said them, and they sounded true, truer than much of what most people ever said. "Maybe he didn't want to put us through what we'd have to endure if he stayed around. A man on alcohol and drugs can cause a lot of trouble for loved ones. Maybe Dad figured leaving might hurt us less than staying. At least with him gone we could get on with our lives."

"That's one way to look at it. "

Allie held the pictures closer. Jack Wilson looked so alive in them, his cockeyed smile, his dimples, his black eyes. She stared into the eyes; they seemed focused straight on her, bored into her psyche. An odd prickly feeling ran up and down her spine, and she almost shuddered.

"Were his eyes as black as they look?" she asked.

Gladys put a hand on Allie's chin and turned it toward her. "His eyes were as black as yours, like hockey pucks," she said. "Never seen anybody with eyes as dark as the two of you."

Allie studied her dad's eyes again. "I've got his eyes," she said.

"I know," Gladys said. "I just never wanted to tell you."

"You think he's still alive?" Allie asked.

"I have no way of knowing."

"I wish I knew one way or the other."

Silence fell on the room for several seconds. Allie finally lowered the picture and faced her mom again. The spell of her dad's eyes had ended.

"You planning on spending the night?" Gladys asked.

"Why not. I'm already in my pajamas."

"Good to have you home."

Allie smiled, hugged her mom, and plopped back into the middle of the mess on the floor, the picture of her dad placed beside the clock radio next to her bed.

"I need to clean up the kitchen," Gladys said.

Allie waved her away, then glanced around her childhood room. "I'm getting married," she said to the walls.

The walls seemed unimpressed.

"Kind of scary."

The walls said nothing.

2

Allie woke the next morning to the sound of music pouring from her radio alarm clock. She rolled over to turn it off, but the radio sat on her dresser five feet away. To turn it off, she had to get out of bed, and she didn't want to do that yet, so she stayed put. Sunshine streamed through the bedroom windows and fell on her face. For a few seconds, she didn't move, just lay still and enjoyed the sun's warmth and the smell of her pillow under her cheek. She heard her mom rumbling around down the hallway and, pretending to be upset, called out to her. "Mom!"

"Yes?"

"Did you set this alarm to go off?"

"No."

"It came on by itself?"

"I guess so."

Allie wrapped her pillow around her ears to shut out the music, but it drifted through anyway, so she put the pillow back under her head and tried to relax. "What's for breakfast?" she called to Gladys.

"Got some pancake mix ready. Just need to throw it in a pan."

Allie rubbed her eyes and tried to decide if she wanted

to get up yet. The music continued, and she tried to ignore it but couldn't. The song's chorus repeated a phrase over and over again.

"Her father's eyes, her father's eyes."

A shot of electricity jolted Allie's spine, and she sat up straight, her back against the headboard. What was this song? The music continued. Allie wondered who had written it and why. The chorus started again.

"She had her father's eyes, her father's eyes."

Unable to listen to any more, Allie rolled out of bed and flipped off the radio. For at least a minute, she stood by the dresser, her body trembling slightly. The picture of her dad lay beside the radio where she'd left it. Her dad gazed up at her, and just as it had happened last night, she felt his eyes boring into her, penetrating, cutting through some shell she'd wrapped around her heart without ever knowing it. She started to pick up the photo but knew she didn't dare.

"Pancakes are almost ready," her mom said as she entered the room, a red apron tied around her waist over tan slacks and a darker brown blouse. "Wash up and come on down."

Allie glanced back at the picture, then set her jaw and headed to the bathroom. A few minutes later, dressed in black heels, black dress pants, and a white silk sweater, she sat down at the kitchen table and picked up the cup of coffee her mom had fixed for her. Gladys brought a plate of pancakes and a bottle of syrup over and plopped them down. Allie took a pancake, poured syrup on it, and began to eat. A cardinal landed on the birdbath just past the back deck, and Allie gazed at it through the window. The cardinal pecked at the food her mom put out every morning.

"You going to the florist after school today?" her mom asked.

"Right after I check on my girls."

Gladys smiled. "You can't practice the team right now, can you?"

"No, but I can make sure they're doing their individual workouts on their own."

Allie and Gladys ate without talking for a couple of minutes. The chorus from the radio kept playing through Allie's head. She tried to push the words away but couldn't.

The cardinal chirped a couple of times and flew away. Allie laid down her fork and stared at her mom. "You ever hear a song named 'Her Father's Eyes' or something like that?" she asked.

Gladys shrugged. "No. Why you ask?"

Allie sipped her coffee and started to tell her mom about the song, but it sounded odd as she rolled it around in her thoughts, so she dropped it. "No reason, not important."

Gladys stared at her for a moment—eyebrows knitted—but then let it go. "You seeing Trey tonight?"

"Yeah, we have to make final decisions about boutonnieres."

"I'm sure he's up for that."

"Trey's up for anything related to this wedding."

"What about his mother?"

Allie smiled slightly. "I think she would rather sit in a tub of scalding butter than have anything to do with any of it."

"I'm sure it's not that bad."

"Least I know it's not me; Trey said she's been against every girl he's ever had any interest in. She wants Trey at home with her forever."

"You ever feel he's just a bit too much of a mama's boy for you?"

Allie studied the question as she munched a pancake. "Mrs. Thompson has been ill a lot," she finally concluded, avoiding the hook in the question. "She needs Trey, says he's all she's got."

Her mom chuckled. "Getting sick is the oldest trick in the book for a mom who wants to keep a child close to home."

Allie set down her coffee cup. "Trey is marrying me three weeks from tomorrow," she said. "Sick mother or not . . . Ruth Thompson will just have to deal."

Gladys wiped her mouth with a cloth napkin, and Allie quickly finished her pancakes, stood, and kissed her on the cheek. "Got to go," Allie said.

"Call me later."

"I'll do it."

The rest of the day passed quickly for Allie. In addition to her coaching during the basketball season, she taught two classes—Marketing 101 and an upper level Advertising and the Media course. At 3:30 she finished up the advertising class and hustled to the gym to check on her team's after-school workouts. Although she couldn't officially coach the girls in the off-season, she still expected them to lift weights four days a week and spend some time on the court shooting and playing informal pickup games.

As expected, she found a number of the girls in the locker room changing into their basketball clothes. One of the girls—a tall redhead named Sarah—stood by a mirror, her index finger shoved toward her left eye. Allie stepped to her and patted her on the back.

"Got a contact lens problem?" she asked Sarah.

"Just got these new ones," Sarah said. "They're bugging me. Needed to clean them."

Sarah pushed the contact toward her eye, set it in place, and positioned the second one on the tip of her finger. Allie looked at Sarah's reflection in the mirror as she arranged the second contact. High cheekbones, dimples, long lashes—a beautiful, five-foot-nine-inch-tall forward who wowed the boys in the hallways of school and took no prisoners under the rims in a basketball game. Sarah caught Allie's eye and smiled.

"Wish I had your eyes," Sarah said.

Allie stepped back a half step. "Your eyes are gorgeous," she said. "Hazel, aren't they?"

"Not as pretty as yours."

Lisa, the starting point guard, walked up. "She's right. You got the best eyes any of us have ever seen."

Allie wanted to melt into the floor and disappear. Not only did she try to avoid talking about looks with her basketball team—comparisons like that never helped anyone, particularly sensitive young women—but she specifically didn't want any attention brought to her eyes right now.

She turned to walk away, but four more girls suddenly appeared beside her, and she knew that leaving right then would feel odd—like the four who had just walked up had run her off or something. The six teammates clustered around Allie, all of them looking into the mirror, opening their eyes wide, pulling at their eyelashes, moistening their lips, checking out their profiles.

Sarah pointed to the point guard's face. "Lisa's got a pretty blue thing going on with her eyes," she said.

Lisa turned to Sarah. "Are yours green?"

"Based on my mood," Sarah said. "Sometimes green, sometimes hazel."

Allie tried to relax and enjoy the chatter of her girls. Nothing quite like the locker room with a bunch of young women to remind her of the reason she loved coaching. Here she got to know her charges, got to influence them in ways nobody else could. Although not religious in any conventional sense, Allie saw the locker room as a holy place, an inner sanctum dedicated to the worship of companionship, teamwork, discipline, and hard work.

"You're Irish, aren't you?" Lisa asked Sarah.

"Halfway at least—on my mama's side. That's where I got my red hair."

Allie figured she could leave now without anybody wondering why. She started to turn.

"Where did you get your eyes?" Lisa asked Allie.

Allie gulped. What was it with all the attention on her eyes in the last twenty-four hours? The same prickly feeling the picture of her dad and the song had caused returned to her spine. This time a slight rise of the hair on her arms also occurred.

"Must be her dad," Sarah said. "I've seen her mom's eyes."

"Yeah, they're kind of grayish," Lisa agreed. "Not black like yours."

"Yours are black as coal," Sarah said.

All six girls focused on Allie, and she wanted to duck and slink away but felt trapped again. The girls stared at her eyes through the mirror, and she knew they expected her to say something, and since she didn't know how to avoid it, she obliged them. "My mom says I have my father's eyes."

"They're fantastic," Lisa said.

Sarah asked the question Allie had hoped nobody would ask. "Does your dad live around here?"

Allie shook her head. "No."

Lisa threw the last punch without even meaning to. "Where does he live?"

Allie patted Lisa on the back. "Get dressed, ladies," she ordered. "I've got things to do, and you do too. I'll check back in on you in an hour or so."

With that, she hustled away from the locker room before anybody could ask any more embarrassing questions she had no clue how to answer.

Allie met Trey for dinner about two hours later at a small Italian restaurant about a mile from her school. He offered her a casual peck on the cheek as she walked up, and she took it, then sat down with him. They ordered quickly—lasagna and salad for him, spaghetti and salad for her.

"How's your mom?" she asked.

"Some better but not a lot."

"I hope she'll feel better by the wedding," she said genuinely but without knowing whether she was really sick or not. A mom giving up her only child to another woman never came easy, especially not to a woman like Ruth Thompson.

"She . . . she mentioned that too," Trey said, his chin downcast. "She said she wanted to be there more than anything and hoped she got stronger before then."

Allie's antenna went up, and she got a little frustrated. "She's trying to scare you," she said.

Trey glanced up, then nodded.

23

"You need to let her know that the wedding goes on regardless."

Trey rubbed his eyes, and Allie felt sorry for him. His mother put him in some hard spots sometimes, came up sick a lot when he and Allie wanted to do something special. More than once they had postponed outings so Trey could stay with his mother through one of her bouts with various illnesses. The last couple of times, Allie had suggested to Trey that they go anyway, that his mother was manipulating him, but he'd refused.

"She's fragile," he explained. "What kind of son leaves his mother when she needs him?"

Unable to argue with that, Allie had dropped her suggestion. Now she took Trey's hands and decided to stay positive, to put all negative thoughts away. No more worry about Ruth Thompson, no more anxiety about her missing dad. Time to talk about the wedding plans—the golf outing Trey had planned for his groomsmen, the menu for the dinner after the ceremony, the vows they would take before the minister at the Methodist church on the main street in Harper Springs.

"One thing we haven't talked about," Trey said, nibbling a bite of salad.

"What's that?"

"Who's going to walk you down the aisle?"

Allie straightened up, surprised that Trey had chosen this particular evening to bring up a question she'd considered a couple of times but then discarded as useless to worry over. As far as she was concerned, she would make her way to the altar alone.

"I know it's not fun to think about," Trey said, reaching for her hand. "I suppose that's why you haven't mentioned it. Not having a dad around at a time like this has to be hard . . . but we do have to ask somebody, don't you think?"

Allie stared past him out the window. "I can walk the aisle by myself," she said. "Or my mom can walk beside me."

"You think that's appropriate?"

"Who's to say? It's my wedding, isn't it?"

"True, but . . ."

Allie sighed, and the picture of her dad rose in her mind again. Deep sadness swept through her. She wanted Jack Wilson to take the trip down the aisle with her more than anything, but what could she do?

She focused on Trey again. "Do you believe in God?" she asked.

Trey leaned back a little. "What's that got to do with anything?"

"Just humor me for a second," she said. "Do you believe in God?"

"Yes, sure, everybody does, don't they?"

"Okay." Allie hesitated, not sure how to say what she needed to voice but knowing she had to get it out. "Let's agree for the moment that God exists. But does God ever try to speak to us, to tell us something we might need to know?"

Trey propped his elbows on the table and intertwined his fingers. "You're asking a crazy question, don't you think?"

Allie recalled the picture from the previous night, the way her dad's eyes seemed so intent, so fixed on her. She quickly told Trey what had happened—the photo she'd found, the song that morning, her girls' comments about her eyes in the locker room. "I feel like somebody, something,

25

a higher power, a cosmic force, God maybe, is trying to get a message to me," she said.

"I've never even heard you mention God," Trey said, his voice rising slightly. "Now you think you're hearing messages from him? Or her. Whichever. You're not about to go all 'Jesus' on me, are you?"

Allie smiled but only briefly. "I know it's bizarre . . . but . . ." She paused, unable to go on, unable to convince herself, much less Trey, of what she was suggesting.

Trey rubbed his chin and shifted into his counseling mode. "Let's pretend for argument's sake that God is talking to you," he offered. "What's the message? That you've got eyes like your daddy? So what? Millions of girls, boys too, can say that."

"It's more than that," Allie insisted, although still not certain of what she was saying, feeling like an ant trying to explain quantum physics. "It's . . . it's . . ."

"It's what?" Trey asked, obviously perturbed.

"I don't know."

The waiter interrupted them with more rolls, and they both leaned back, almost as if agreeing to take a break from the intensity of the conversation.

Trey locked his fingers again. "Look," he said, "every girl wants her dad to walk her down the aisle. But you won't get to experience that. You should expect to feel some sadness about it. You should expect that your missing father will become important to you right now."

"But what about the feeling I had when I saw the picture last night, the song, the girls? Even your bringing up the fact that my dad won't be walking me down the aisle?"

"A series of strange coincidences," Trey said. "Nothing more, nothing less."

"So you don't believe God is trying to tell me something?"

Trey chuckled. "I believe in Sigmund Freud," he said. "Carl Jung too, maybe even B. F. Skinner if you catch me on a bad day. I believe in the science of psychology. Your subconscious is talking to you, that's all. You want your dad with you at this transition point in your life, and you've found this picture, and now you're interpreting everything that happens through the lens of your loneliness. But God talking to you, a celestial message from on high? Come on. Just because you heard a song and some high school girls commented on your eyes—and they are magnificent, by the way—don't go off half-cocked and get all mysterious on me. It's not like you."

Allie took a sip of water and realized Trey held the logic card, and it trumped all her coincidences.

"I know you're right," she said. "I've never thought of God in any personal sense. It's not that Mom and I don't go to church every now and again—every Easter and Christmas we show up at Main Street Methodist."

"You told me you went through confirmation classes too."

"When I was twelve. But God has always seemed pretty remote, a spiritual ooze of some sort—ill-defined and absent, not more than that."

Trey nodded. "Same here," he said. "I believe God exists, I guess . . . but doesn't get much involved in what happens to individual humans."

"Yeah," she agreed, eager to say out loud what she had always felt but rarely expressed. "Like a cosmic engineer or something, somebody who tinkered the universe into being but then left it alone."

Silence fell for a moment, and Trey took a deep breath. "I'm sorry I got a little defensive when you mentioned God," he said, "but I've seen some bad examples of what religion can do to people. Makes some folks almost scary they get so wrapped up in it."

"It's probably not the best thing to throw on you just before the wedding."

"Religion can get tricky."

"And you've never seen much of it in me."

"Exactly. I'm not opposed to it, mind you, just not in big doses."

Allie picked up a roll. The waiter checked on them, but they told him they were fine. Allie took a bite of her roll, then put it back on her plate. "I don't even know if he's alive or dead," she said softly.

"Your dad?"

"Yes."

"Wouldn't your mom have gotten some notification or something if he had died?"

"Maybe, but what if he had nothing on him to indicate he was even married?"

"You got me there."

"I just wish I knew one way or the other."

"I know it's tough," Trey said. "My dad's gone too. You know that."

"At least you know where he is," she said. "Out at Greenview Cemetery overlooking the valley below Harper Springs, row twenty-six, right by the stand of pines."

Trey took a bite of lasagna, and Allie took his hand. She knew the story; his mother made sure everyone knew it, how she'd struggled and scrimped and sacrificed to put Trey through NC State after his dad died of a heart attack.

"So who should do it?" she asked.

"Do what?"

"Walk me down the aisle."

"Your uncle Todd?"

Allie pondered the suggestion. Her mom's brother Todd had taught her how to shoot a basketball. "That's a good idea," she said.

"I'm sure he'd be honored."

Allie took a bite of salad, and they began to talk about the wedding again. Before she knew it, they'd finished their meal, Trey had kissed her good night at her car, and she'd driven back home, her mind calmer but not completely settled about much of anything, much less the matter of whether or not she believed in a God who actually tried to talk to people through pictures or songs or basketball players or anything else.

Two hours later, after eating two chocolate chip cookies with milk, Allie brushed her teeth, crawled into bed, and flipped on the television with the remote control. For several minutes she flipped aimlessly from channel to channel, hoping to see something to distract her from the troubling thoughts that kept racing through her mind. Every now and again, she glanced at the picture of her and her dad, which now sat on her bedside table. Every time she looked, she felt foolish, like a woman who had just found out she'd walked around all day with old chewing gum stuck to the back of her pants. The television controls landed on a documentary about the advent of television commercials, and she halted her channel surfing for a moment to take a look. A parade of old black-and-white images flashed across the screen.

"Plop, plop, fizz, fizz. Oh what a relief it is. Alka Seltzer."

Allie smiled as she watched the classic ad and listened to the somber voice of the narrator as he spoke of the medicine's effect.

When that ad ended, a blond boy appeared on-screen. He stood at the front door of a house and asked the woman standing at the door if a friend could come out to play. The mother explained that the friend had a fever and she had given him Bayer aspirin to make him feel better.

The boy's sweet voice concluded the spot. "Mothers are like that . . . yeah, they are."

What a timeless promo! A couple of others Allie didn't recognize flashed across the television, and she almost flipped away to find something else. Then the face of a dark-haired woman with long black eyelashes filled the television screen, and Allie halted.

The woman's eyes expanded as she lifted a brush to her eyelashes as she stared into a mirror.

The sounds of a jingle played in the background.

The hair on the back of Allie's neck stood up, her body tingled, and she held her breath.

"Jeepers creepers. Where'd you get them peepers? Jeepers creepers. Where'd ya get those eyes?"

Allie almost screamed as the ad ended and the station went to a commercial. Her breath came in ragged gulps, and she dropped her feet to the floor and stood, not sure where she was going but knowing she had to move, had to do something to shake off the sense of weirdness she felt.

Her cat, Patch, a gray stray who had shown up at her doorstep about a year ago, suddenly padded into the room and jumped onto her bed.

"It's too much!" Allie muttered, picking Patch up. "Too much!"

She rubbed Patch's stomach and tried to figure it all out. In spite of Trey's confidence about coincidences, she didn't see how everything that had happened in the last twenty-four hours could be connected by nothing more than random chance. Somebody—she didn't necessarily want to say God, but somebody—or something wanted her to pay attention. But what was the message?

Allie carried Patch to the kitchen, poured some cat food into her bowl, and dropped her to the floor. Then she moved to the cabinet, pulled out the cookies, and lifted two more from the pack.

"I'm not going to fit in my wedding dress," she told Patch as she munched a cookie.

Busy with her own food, Patch seemed to have little interest in the effects of the cookies upon Allie's waistline.

Carrying the second cookie with her, Allie moved to the small deck just outside her kitchen door. For a long time, she stared into the woods past her yard. Stars twinkled overhead, and she finished the cookie and gazed into the heavens. Below her the little town of Harper Springs—all three thousand people of it, all mountains in the distance and blue haze in the late afternoons—blinked its lights up at her.

"What?" she said into the night air. "What am I supposed to hear in all this?"

Nobody answered.

Allie left the deck, eased back to her bedroom, and picked up the picture of her and her dad.

"I'm listening," she said to the picture. Again she got no response.

Still holding the picture, she moved to the deck once more, propped her elbows on the railing, and squinted at her dad's face. The light from the kitchen seeped through the window and lit up his eyes. They penetrated through the shadows and burned a hole in her head and heart, and Allie suddenly knew what she had to do. In spite of Trey's irrefutable logic and her own doubts, she knew that something greater than reason now beckoned her. Although she didn't know what it was—her own subconscious, the spirit of her dad, God, whatever—she had to respond to the summons or forever wonder what she'd missed by ignoring it.

"Okay," she said to the picture, a sense of excitement mixed with fear rising in her bones. "You win."

The picture said nothing.

"Tomorrow," Allie whispered. "Tomorrow I'll start looking."

Patch slid through the open door and rubbed against the back of Allie's legs. Allie turned and picked her up. "Everybody will think I've lost my mind," she whispered to Patch.

Patch stared into the dark, obviously content to let everybody think whatever they wanted. Standing on the back deck as the spring breeze fingered her face, Allie felt a sense of peace and knew she'd made the right decision. Insane or not, before she walked down the aisle to marry Trey, she had to know what had happened to her dad and what message she was supposed to learn from it.

SECTION 2

The search for truth is the most important work in the whole world, and the most dangerous.

James Clavell

3

Allie woke up early on Saturday, showered, ate a bowl of cereal, and called her school principal at his home right after eight and told him she needed to take the rest of the year off. He needed to get a substitute for her.

"Getting last minute things ready for the wedding?" he asked.

"You could say that."

"You were already going to be out the last week, weren't you?"

"Yes, a substitute is already lined up for that."

"Then it's just a week."

"Yes."

"Okay, you've got more than enough time built up. No problem."

After she hung up, she dressed quickly in jeans, a University of North Carolina T-shirt, and running shoes and drove straight to her mother's house. Although she didn't plan to come right out and tell Gladys what she hoped to do, she did need her help digging around.

She found her mom wearing a wide-brimmed straw hat and gloves in the flower patch of her front yard. Sweat poured down Gladys's face as she pulled weeds. She stood and wiped her brow as Allie climbed out of her white SUV.

"You're out early," Gladys said.

"Lots to do."

Gladys slipped off her gloves, left the garden, and led her into the kitchen. Allie poured two glasses of orange juice and set them on the table. Gladys pulled out a couple of muffins and placed them on a plate. Both women sat down.

"You got something on your mind," Gladys said, taking a swig of juice.

"What makes you say that?"

"Wild horses couldn't usually pull you out of bed on Saturday until at least ten."

Allie nibbled a muffin, then said, "That picture of you and Dad—who are the other folks in it?"

"Beth and Walt Mason, our best friends at the time—your dad grew up with Walt. Played baseball with him in school. They had a little band too; your dad picked the electric guitar some. Then they went to Vietnam together. "

"Mrs. Mason a friend of yours?"

"Only through Walt and your dad."

Allie drank some juice. "You know where Mr. and Mrs. Mason are now?"

"Why you ask?"

Allie wasn't sure how to proceed without risking upsetting her mom, but she didn't see any other choice but to go ahead. "I thought I might call them or something. See if they know where Dad might be, what happened to him."

Gladys shifted, raised an eyebrow. "I don't see how digging up old bones that have long since decayed can be a good idea."

A touch of anger rose in Allie. How could her mom not care more than she did? "Don't you ever wonder what happened to him?" she asked.

"Every day of my life."

"Then why don't you do something about it?"

Gladys nibbled her muffin. "I tried at first," she said quietly. "Called every friend of his I knew—a few I didn't. Spent money I didn't have taking a couple of trips to places he'd mentioned he wanted to visit someday—down to Orlando, up to Nashville."

"No sign of him anywhere?"

"Not a trace; it was like he'd dropped off the face of the earth. After a while, I decided your dad didn't want me to find him. Why else would he leave like he did? I figured it best to follow his wishes and let him be."

Allie tried to soak it all in. After all these years, she and her mom were finally talking about something they should have addressed years ago. "I'm sorry he left you," she said.

"It's been hard on both of us."

Allie's eyes watered as she realized she'd focused on her own loss so much that she'd largely forgotten her mom's. "Thanks for the way you've provided for me," she said.

Gladys waved her off. "You're the best thing I ever did," she said.

Allie touched Gladys's arm, then leaned back and took a bite of muffin.

"Walt and Beth lived in Knoxville for a while," Gladys said.

"You have an address?"

"They sent Christmas cards for years. Maybe I've got one stuck away somewhere with an address on it."

"You mind if I look for it?"

"I already said I'd advise against contacting them."

"I don't see how a phone call can hurt anything. Dad might have visited them over the years, phoned or something."

"What will you do if you find out he did?"

Allie paused, not sure how to answer.

Gladys leaned closer. "Look," she said. "Your dad left us. It's a hard truth to hear, but you've known it all your life. What's so urgent right now—right before your wedding—that causes you to go scraping around in the past? Nothing good can come of it. I know that as certain as I know this muffin—" she held hers up "—is a day past stale."

Allie rubbed her eyes, again not sure what to say and what to keep silent. Would her mom think her addled if she said what she was thinking? But how could she keep it quiet? Before she could change her mind, Allie told her about the odd happenings over the past day and a half, how everything focused on the resemblance between her eyes and her dad's. Gladys listened quietly, then chuckled a little as Allie finished the tale.

"Sounds like *X-Files* stuff," Gladys said. "Psychic phenomena."

"You're telling me."

"If you know it's bizarre, why dwell on it?"

Allie sighed. "I've been asking myself the same thing, but . . . I don't know . . . I just feel I have to see what I can find out; it's like a hand pulling at my belt, yanking me toward it."

"Have you talked to Trey about this?"

Allie told her about her conversation with Trey and how he'd responded.

"I think I'd tend to agree with him," Gladys said. "It's a bunch of odd happenings, that's it."

In spite of the logic on her mom's side, Allie still felt her jaw setting. "It's more than that," she insisted.

"I raised you better than to go off half-cocked like this," Gladys argued. "Taught you to use your head, be rational."

"Maybe it's ESP or something," Allie said, ignoring her. "Maybe Dad is in trouble; he needs me and is sending me a message."

"You're talking hocus-pocus."

"You don't believe in anything like that . . . anything supernatural?" The word sounded strange on her tongue, spooky even.

Gladys looked at her hands, calloused from the yard work that kept her busy most of the time when she wasn't working at the department store office she managed. "No," she said. "I don't."

"No belief in God at all?"

"None that makes any difference in my life."

"But we go to church sometimes. You put me through confirmation."

Gladys shrugged. "A little religion is fine," she said, "and I wish I did believe, could believe. It might have made things easier, helped me find some explanation for what your dad did. But those answers never came, not from God or anyone else."

"But didn't your folks take you to church when you were a child?"

"A good bit. Solid Methodist people, my mom and dad. But God never did enough for me to give me any reason to really believe. Took both of them early, and then your dad disappeared."

Allie nodded sympathetically. Her mom's parents had

both died early—her dad from a car accident involving a teenager on drugs and her mom from cancer. Although an aunt on her mom's side had done the best she could raising Gladys, money was scarce, and Gladys took her first job at twelve at the Cut and Dried Hair Salon and never looked back. For the most part, except for the years Jack was around, Gladys had survived largely by her own efforts. She paid for community college by working lots of hours. She had a degree in accounting and a solid job. She'd never been wealthy, but in Harper Springs a little money stretched a long way.

"I don't know that God has a thing to do with what's happening to me," Allie said, "but I still want to contact the Masons if I can."

Gladys drank from her juice, then set down the glass. "You're a grown woman. Do what you want. I'll see if I can find the address, and maybe you can track down a phone number from it."

"Thank you."

"You plan to tell Trey what you're up to?"

Allie weighed the question. "I don't want to deceive him in any way," she said.

"Then you best talk to him soon as you can."

"I will."

"I'd like to be a fly on the wall when that conversation happens."

"He'll be fine; he's an understanding man."

"You about finished with that house?"

"A lot of work yet to go."

"He may be understanding, but his mama might not be."

"I can't live my life worried about what Ruth Thompson is going to think of me."

Gladys lifted an eyebrow, and Allie took her hands and held them close. A question arose that she'd never even considered but now felt she couldn't avoid. "Why didn't you divorce him, Mom?"

Gladys shrugged. "I took vows," she said. "'Till death do us part' meant something to me."

"But you just told me you're not religious."

"A vow is a vow; religion has nothing to do with it."

Allie searched her mom's face and saw something she'd never before realized. "You still love him, don't you?"

Gladys covered her mouth with her hand, and tiny tears glinted in her eyes as she nodded quietly.

"I admire you for that," Allie whispered. "That's why you never remarried, isn't it?"

Again Gladys nodded. "You better love Trey the same way," she said, wiping her eyes. "You marry a man, you better love him enough to stay with him come what may."

Allie swallowed hard, the seriousness of what she would do in just three weeks settling over her. But why should she worry? She loved Trey just as much as her mom loved her dad, didn't she? Nothing could come between them that would ever make her want to leave him, could it? But who knew what life might bring? What if Trey treated her as poorly as her dad treated her mom? Could she still love him after all that?

Allie shuddered, then pushed the scary questions away. The morning sun warmed her face through the kitchen window. "I really do believe dad is trying to tell me something," she said softly.

"If you're right, I just hope it's something good."

"Me too, Mom. Me too."

It took Gladys until late that evening to find the address, so Allie waited until Sunday morning after ten to call directory information in Knoxville. The operator told her she didn't have a Walt or a Beth Mason, but she did have the number for a Walter Mason III. Not knowing what else to do, Allie wrote down the number and tried to call it four times between ten and one. To her dismay, she reached a computerized voice message every time, one of those that gave her no clue whether or not she'd actually reached the right people. For the rest of the day, she called back every chance she got but had no luck. Finally she left a message with her number and her mom's. She met Trey at six for dinner, ate a light supper, and talked about the hotel arrangements for the guests coming from out of town. Apparently, a couple of the guests had discovered some trouble making online reservations, and Trey had spent several hours that day trying to get it all straightened out.

Although she tried to focus, Allie found herself distracted for most of the evening and offered Trey little help. Finally they said their good-byes, and she drove back home. In her bedroom she started to call the Masons again but then decided it was inappropriate since it was past eleven o'clock. Feeling frustrated, she pulled out some old stationery, sat down at her kitchen table with a glass of tea, and scratched out a letter to Walt and Beth Mason.

Dear Mr. and Mrs. Mason,
   I hope this letter reaches you both and finds you well. Perhaps you won't remember me, but I'm

the daughter of Gladys Wilson, over in Harper Springs, North Carolina. You were friends of my dad, Jack Wilson—perhaps you still are.

That's why I'm writing you now, out of the blue.

I'm trying to find out what happened to my dad, where I might get in touch with him, if he's still alive—I don't even know that.

If you have any information about him, would you please respond by calling me collect at 423-771-2260 or by emailing me at AWilson@abc.com? You can, of course, write me back if that's easiest for you.

Thank you for your help, and perhaps I can meet you sometime in the future.

Satisfied that she'd done all she could for the day, Allie signed the letter, addressed it, slapped a stamp on it, and left it in her mailbox for Monday pickup. Back in her apartment, she put on her pajamas, grown-up tan ones with no patterns this time, and climbed into bed. Patch jumped up beside her and snuggled down. Allie closed her eyes but found it hard to sleep. The image of her dad kept popping into her head—the eyes, always the eyes, staring at her.

What? she wondered. *What are you trying to tell me?*

She thought of Trey and considered the idea that some latent fear about marrying him had pushed up from her subconscious to make her go off on this wild goose chase but quickly dismissed the idea. Trey and she loved each other; they were the right age, it was the right time, everyone agreed they fit. Marriage with Trey made sense; she knew it as well as she knew that Patch had spots of black all over her. But if it wasn't something about Trey, then what was it?

For the next two hours, Allie tossed and rolled under her covers and pulled her pillow over her head. Patch jumped to the floor and left the room after a while, obviously disturbed by her hyperactivity. Allie tried listening to some music, half expecting some lyrics about eyes to pour through the radio speakers, but thankfully, nothing of the sort happened.

Calming a little, Allie decided what she needed to do. Give it a few days, she concluded. Let her letter to the Masons go out; give them time to write her back. Until then there was nothing else she could do. Finally satisfied, she calmed herself enough to slip into a troubled sleep.

4

Allie spent Monday through Friday of the next week trying to focus on wedding matters. Since Trey's mother had given them a cottage-style, three-bedroom house that had all the basics in place but needed a great deal of renovation, she worked for hours each day to help redo it. She donned old jeans and a sweatshirt to aid the painters Trey had hired, gave directions to the carpenters repairing the front porch where a column had rotted out, and watched anxiously as a flooring team put down new carpet, tile, and hardwood. In addition, the windows needed new drapes, the bathrooms completely new fixtures, and the kitchen new countertops and cabinets. She saw Trey every day after he left his office, but they didn't talk much about anything but the most immediate concerns—the caterer wanted to charge them two dollars more per plate than originally agreed upon, one of the groomsmen had an emergency at the bank where he worked and didn't know if he could make the wedding, and the airline company through which they had booked their honeymoon flight to Cancun had gone bankrupt and they needed to switch their tickets to another carrier. By

Friday Allie wanted to pull her hair out; how did anyone ever get through the last minute wedding plan snafus?

As busy as she was, though, Allie's thoughts never drifted far from the letter she'd sent to the Masons. Every day when she got home, she rushed to her answering machine to see if they'd called. When she came up empty there, she moved to her email messages but again found nothing. On Thursday she'd started checking her mailbox for a letter. If the Masons got her letter on Tuesday—Wednesday at the latest—and wrote back the same day, a letter might have reached her by Thursday. But she found no letter of response. She also repeatedly called the phone number the operator had given her, but the same computerized voice sounded back every time.

By Friday Allie had almost decided to let it all drop. If her dad was trying to beam some telepathic message to her through songs, television documentaries, and high-school girls' basketball teams, why didn't he also show her how to get in touch with him? Or if it was God wanting to snatch her attention—no, she didn't really think that—but if so, why couldn't God make it a little easier to move forward?

Allie tried the phone one more time late Friday but once more reached nothing but the computerized voice. She slammed down the phone and stood in her bedroom, her jaw clenched in frustration. Patch eased up to her ankles and rubbed against her.

"I'm done," Allie said, picking Patch up. "I don't know what else to do."

Patch purred and licked her lips.

The phone rang. Allie jumped back and stared at the phone. It rang again. Patch looked at her as if to ask, "Aren't you going to answer?"

Her hand trembling a little, Allie reached for the phone. Her mom answered when she said hello. Allie sighed heavily, disappointed and yet also relieved. What had she expected? A bolt of lightning, a last-minute call to give her directions on her absurd quest? Craziness, she concluded, premarriage jitters causing her to go off the beam for a few days.

"What are you doing?" Gladys asked.

"Just walked in from the house—been cleaning out the basement all day."

"Anything I can help do?"

"You know how to grout?"

"Not sure what grout is."

"I do, and you're wise to stick to that story as long as you can."

Conversation paused for a moment. Allie sensed something in the silence. Her mom was holding something back. "What's going on?" she probed.

"I got a call," Gladys said.

"What kind of call?"

"From Knoxville."

Allie held her breath. "The Masons?" she asked.

"No."

"Then who?"

"Their son, Chase."

"What did he say?"

"His parents are traveling in Europe right now. He goes by their house every few days to check on things, pick up their mail, monitor their phone messages."

Allie's shoulders slumped. Although she'd considered giving up her search, disappointment still ate through her. If she didn't find out about her dad now, she sensed she never would. Life would get too busy after her marriage; too many other things to call her away from some silly notion of locating her dad.

"Why did he call you and not me?" she asked, slightly perturbed.

"He said he tried you first, but no answer."

Allie dropped Patch and moved to her window. "Did he say when his folks will come home?"

"Yeah, he expects them back the end of next week. He said he heard your message and found your letter. Wanted to know if this was some kind of emergency or something."

Allie stared into the oak trees past her window for several moments and wondered the same thing. Was this an emergency—a once-in-a-life sliver of time that demanded an action that if not taken would be lost forever?

"I guess this is the end of it?" Gladys offered.

Allie weighed the matter and surprised herself when she answered. "Did Mr. Mason leave a number?" she asked.

"Well, yes, he did. Said if it was an emergency, call him back. You're not figuring on doing that, are you?"

Allie stayed quiet.

"Look, the Masons aren't available. You have a wedding in two weeks. I've indulged you to this point, but enough is enough. If you want to contact the Masons when you get back from your honeymoon, fine. I'll support that. But you've got to drop this for now; you know it as well as I do."

"Just give me his number," Allie said. "I'll make one call."

"What do you think he can tell you?"

"I don't know, but I've got to try."

"No, you don't."

"Yes, I do."

Gladys started to speak again, but Allie interrupted her. "Mom, you said yourself, I'm a grown woman. If I want to do this, you have no right to stop me."

"Not even if I think you're being foolish?"

"Not even then."

"Okay," Gladys said. "Here's the number."

Allie grabbed a pen, wrote down the number, thanked her mom, and hung up. Not even hesitating, she punched in the number. Seconds later a male voice answered, a voice deeper than any she'd ever heard, like the man had found it on the bottom of the Mississippi River.

"Is this Chase Mason?" she asked, her heart racing.

"It is."

"This is Allie Wilson; I sent your folks a letter."

"You called too, several times." The voice sounded warm in spite of its depth, a voice that immediately inspired respect, maybe even awe.

Allie wondered what he looked like.

"You're trying to reach my folks," he said.

"Yes."

"Is it an emergency?"

Allie hesitated, not sure how to respond. "Have you read the letter I sent?"

Chase chuckled, and Allie felt like the phone rumbled from the sound. "No," he said. "I don't read other people's mail; it's a crime, I think."

"I need to talk to your folks," she said, feeling embarrassed for reasons she couldn't quite understand.

"I'm not sure exactly where to reach them," he said. "They've been in France, Spain, all over the place. Kind of a lifelong dream trip finally come true."

"You have a phone number where I can call them?"

"Not really. They call me every few days, not the other way around. They're in one place today, another tomorrow."

Allie's frustration rose, and she spoke before she could stop herself. "You don't know how to reach your mom and dad?"

"They're grown-ups." He laughed gently. "In an emergency I can track them down, I suppose; otherwise, I expect they're old enough to make it on their own."

Allie bit her lip and told herself to calm down. "It's not an emergency," she said.

"Okay, then."

Allie knew she should say good-bye and hang up, but something kept her on the line.

"Anything else I can do for you?" Chase asked.

"Read the letter I sent," Allie said quickly.

"What?"

"The letter; you still have it?"

"Yeah, with my folks' mail."

"I want you to read it."

"You're sure?"

"Yes, please."

"Okay, hang on a sec."

Allie sat down at the kitchen table and waited while Chase left the phone. Patch lay down on her feet and yawned. Chase returned to the line.

"I've got the letter," he said, his tone easy.

"Read it," Allie ordered him.

Again silence. Allie picked Patch up and held her.

A minute later Chase broke the quiet. "I'll help you track my parents down if you want," he said softly.

Allie almost said yes, but she then remembered her manners. "Maybe I shouldn't bother them on their trip," she said.

"I'm sure they won't mind, given the nature of your call."

Allie suddenly got cold feet. Bothering the Masons on their trip seemed odd, out of place, almost kooky. What would she say if she reached them— "Hey, I recently received a revelation from God, and it told me to begin a quest to find my father"? They'd consider her stark raving mad.

"I think I'll just wait until they return," she offered.

"I'll have them call you the minute they reach Knoxville."

"I hope they get back before the wedding," she said. "I'm getting married in a couple of weeks."

"Congratulations."

"Thank you."

Allie's mind locked, and she didn't know what else to say, yet she couldn't bring herself to hang up. Something about Chase's manner, the soothing in his voice, comforted her and made her want to stay on the line.

"I've got an idea," he said gently.

"What?"

"Why don't you run over here to Knoxville, and we'll talk."

"Why would I want to do that?"

"You want to know about your dad, don't you?"

"But your folks aren't there."

"That's true, but I am."

Allie's fingers gripped the phone more tightly. "I don't understand."

"I called him Uncle Jack," Chase said.

"What?"

"Your dad. I knew him, called him Uncle Jack."

Allie dropped Patch on the floor. "You knew my dad?"

"Yes."

"When did you last see him?"

"I think you need to come to Knoxville."

"I don't understand."

"Just come."

Allie wanted to say no but couldn't. Neither, however, could she just hop in a car and drive to Knoxville without more reason than this. "When did you last see my dad?" she asked.

Chase hesitated but then said, "About a year ago."

Allie's head suddenly ached. Her dad had come that close to her but hadn't visited her! "How was he?"

"Come see me, and we'll talk."

Allie considered her plans for Saturday, thought about what she would tell Trey, how she would explain a trip to Knoxville. He wouldn't understand, she knew that, and if his mother found out . . . she didn't even want to imagine the grief he, then she, would receive. Yet how could she refuse to go? She'd discovered someone who knew her dad, someone who had seen him! She easily made her decision.

"What about tomorrow?" Allie asked.

"That'll be fine."

"About noon okay?"

"Fine by me."

"How do I get there?"

Chase gave her directions to an address off I-40, and she jotted them down.

"See you then," he said.

Allie hung up and dropped her head on the table. Patch eased up, and Allie took her into her arms. "What am I doing?" she asked the cat.

Patch yawned, obviously as uncertain as she.

"What will I tell Trey?" she asked. "Or Mom?"

Patch licked a paw, and Allie rubbed her behind the ears. Without quite knowing why, she sensed that tomorrow she would find out something that would change her life forever. For the better or worse, though, she had no way to know, no way at all.

SECTION 3

When people are true friends, even shared water tastes sweet.

Chinese proverb

5

Gladys didn't think much of Allie's plan to go to Knoxville when she called to tell her about it the next morning.

"You got two weeks until your wedding," Gladys said.

"It's half a day," Allie said. "I'm there and back before dinner."

"You don't have a half a day to spare," Gladys argued.

Allie thanked her for her concern and hung up. Although she respected her mom, she didn't always follow her advice.

Thirty minutes later she met Trey at his school for a morning walk before breakfast. Sliding into step with him around the school track, Allie tried to calm down.

"Tile for the bathrooms at the house came in yesterday," Trey said.

"Good."

Trey smiled, and Allie decided she might as well plow right into it. "I'm going to Knoxville when we're done here," she said.

Trey glanced at her but kept walking. "I'm sure you have ample reason."

"I do." She told him about the conversation with Chase Mason.

Trey's pace picked up a little. "What can Mr. Mason tell you in person that he couldn't say over the phone?" he asked.

"I'm not sure."

"Did you ask him that question?"

"No."

Trey's arms pumped at his side. "Where are you meeting Mr. Mason?"

"His place; he gave me an address."

"Do you think that wise?"

"I don't understand."

Trey stopped dead in place and stared at her as she stopped too. "You're so naïve; that's one of the things I love about you. But what do you know about this man? The world is stuffed with lunatics; how do you know he's not going to lure you somewhere and . . . you know what I mean."

"That's absurd. He sounded . . ." She remembered Chase's voice and felt relaxed just thinking about it.

"Absurd or not, I don't like the idea of you running off to meet with another man."

"Are you jealous, Trey?"

He started walking again, her beside him. "Why don't you just call Mr. Mason back. Ask him anything you want, but not in Knoxville," he suggested.

She considered the notion but then discarded it. "Mr. Mason is safe," she said. "I'm sure of it."

Trey's tone notched up a bit. "It's a waste of time," he said. "A wild goose chase."

"Probably, but I have to do it." She had a fresh thought. "Why don't you come with me?"

"I don't have time. You know that. We have to finish the house, and if you're not going to be helping . . ." He let the implication hang in the air.

"It's half a day," she said, exasperated at his lack of support.

"It's a useless trip," he said between clenched teeth. "We both know it."

"I would think you'd want me to find out all I can about my dad!" Allie's frustration boiled over.

Trey walked faster, and when he spoke, he sounded like a parent talking to a child, formal and stiff. "I am certainly supportive of you knowing as much as possible about your father. But what I cannot fathom is why now, two weeks before our marriage, you suddenly find yourself in the throes of what even the most spontaneous person would surely see as a useless pursuit."

Allie tried to figure out a way to make him understand, but nothing came to her. Trey believed in the tangible, not the transcendent, and no matter what she said, he wouldn't change his mind. He'd already declared her collection of events mere coincidences, and nothing she could say would convince him otherwise.

"I have to go," she said, looking at him again. "That's all I can say." He stopped again and stared at her as if watching an alien to see what it would do next.

"What if you find him?" he asked.

"What?"

"Take this to its end point, what you see now as its best conclusion. Suppose you do find a clue that leads you to your dad?"

Allie studied her shoes and his question. Surprisingly, she hadn't really thought much about the end of a successful search. "I . . . I'm not sure," she said. "I'd talk to my dad . . . I know that, but . . . after that . . ."

"Exactly. You're so illogical. You're heading off to Knoxville in hopes of discovering information to reach a father you don't even remember except through a picture you uncovered a few days ago, yet you've not thought about what you'll say when and if you find him. The fact is—and I'm sure I'm right on this—you haven't even thought about what you'll do if Mr. Mason gives you an address for your father today. Have you? Are you going immediately to see him?"

He waited for an answer, and Allie didn't like the sensation of being put on the spot, not one bit. A note of anger rose in her throat, yet she had to admit Trey had called it correctly. She hadn't planned anything past the visit with Chase Mason. If he told her something that might take her another step closer to her dad, she didn't know for sure that she would take that step. Especially not now, so close to her wedding.

"Did you ever consider that maybe your father doesn't want to be found?" Trey asked.

Allie noticed a little smugness in his face. "Why wouldn't he want to be found?" she asked.

"If he wanted to be found, why hasn't he come home?"

"Maybe he didn't want to be found, but he does now."

Trey chuckled and walked again, slowly this time. "Yes, you've told me all about the signs. The universe is talking to you, sending you mysterious messages. Do-do-do-do-do-do-do-do . . . it's *Twilight Zone* time in Harper Springs, North Carolina."

"You don't have to make fun of me."

Trey glanced over at her. "I'm trying to show you how silly you sound, that's all. Your naïveté has gone far enough, don't you think?"

She hesitated; perhaps Trey had it right. But then he spoke again and made her so mad she wanted to spit.

"Your dad is gone," he said. "It's time to put him in the vault, behind you, forever."

Allie rebelled against the words. She could never put her dad behind her, at least not until she walked this last path to try to find him. This time she stopped walking. "I'll be back this afternoon," she snapped.

"Go on, then!" Trey said, waving her away.

Allie reached for his hand, concerned by his anger. "Don't be mad."

"Of course I'm mad."

"But you'll forgive me?"

He wiped his brow. "We'll go to dinner tonight," he said.

"I'll call you soon as I get in."

"I'll be working at the house. Mother wants to see it as soon as we're finished with it."

"I'm sorry I can't help you today."

She kissed him on the cheek and left the track and headed to her car. She and Trey had dealt with disagreements before; they could certainly deal with this one.

Allie found Chase Mason's house—a two-story, white farmhouse with a wide porch—before noon. It nestled snugly into the hillside of a tree-lined valley about twenty miles southeast of Knoxville. A gravel driveway lined by a white picket fence and an eclectic mix of budding trees led to the house, and a yellow dog of questionable breeding wearing a big grin with sharp teeth greeted her as she pulled to a stop. Before she stepped out of the car, the house's front door popped open, and a man the size of a pro linebacker stepped out. He wore blue jeans, tan work boots, and a blue long-sleeved shirt. A white baseball cap with "Volunteers" written in orange covered dark hair that touched on his shirt collar. Allie opened her door, and the man met her as she climbed out.

"Chase Mason," he said, extending his hand.

"Allie Wilson."

His hand felt like granite, the calluses thick in the palm. Allie dropped his hand and gazed around the place. A freshly painted red barn sat to the left, a stone well to the right. The air smelled clean—slightly moist and alive with the fresh growth of the fields around the house. A light breeze played with her hair.

The dog edged toward her, but Chase eased him away with a boot. "Come on in," he said, indicating the house.

In spite of Trey's warning about lunatics, something in Chase immediately made Allie comfortable, and she quickly followed as he led her inside, the dog trailing. Her heels clicked on the hardwood floors as she walked through the entryway and into the den. A stone fireplace with a small fire burning filled the wall opposite her. A simple but well-crafted wood cross hung on the wall above the mantel. A variety of antique furniture decorated the room—a grandfather clock as tall as Chase in one corner, two different china cabinets, a sideboard, a hat rack, a rolltop desk—each of them carved with inlaid wood and festooned with brass handles.

Chase pointed her to a sofa that looked like an antique,

and she sat down. A stack of books lay on a table by the sofa, and she quickly scanned the titles—a couple of novels, a book of poems by Robert Frost, a hardcover copy of a Bible.

"You want something to drink?" Chase offered. "Water, juice?"

She waved him off. "I'm good."

He sat in a rocking chair, pulled off his hat, and placed it on his knee. His hair, thick and a little curly, sprang out and framed his blue eyes. Allie studied his face—a square jaw, a thick forehead, broad cheeks—a solid man in every respect. He looked about her age, maybe a couple of years older. She scanned the room for signs of other people but saw none. No pictures of a wife or children anywhere.

"Thanks for seeing me," she said, not sure how to start the conversation.

"You sounded a little tense last night," he said, his eyes gentle, about the only soft thing on him.

"I am. There's a lot going on . . ."

"Yeah, a wedding is about as tense as it gets."

Allie wanted to ask him if he had a wife but felt it inappropriate, so she kept quiet. Chase's dog dropped down at her feet as if visiting with his best friend. Chase cleared his throat, and Allie again felt stumped about what to say.

"I guess you think I'm a little nutty," she finally said. "Trying to find my dad this close to my wedding."

Chase laughed. "Weddings can make people more than a little nutty," he said. "That woman in Atlanta who ran away from her fiancé the week of the wedding . . . now, that's nutty."

Allie laughed and again wanted to ask him about a wife but didn't. "My fiancé is a psychologist," she said. "He thinks it's normal for a person to want to put missing pieces together before such a major event. He says that's what I'm doing."

"Sounds about right to me, I guess."

Allie wondered if she should tell him about the odd events of the last couple of weeks, then decided, why not? She'd never see Chase Mason again after today; what difference did it make if he thought her strange?

She leaned forward. "Do you believe in signs, Mr. Mason?"

"Call me Chase."

She nodded. "Do you?"

"What kind of signs?" He fingered the cap on his knee.

She quickly told him everything that had happened. It sounded weird coming out, and by the time she finished, her face had turned a little red with embarrassment and she half expected Chase to laugh and ask her to leave. To her surprise, he did nothing of the sort but instead shoved on his cap, stood, reached for her hand to help her up, and told her to follow him.

"Where are we going?" she asked.

"Upstairs," he said.

She dug in her heels, and he stopped, turned, and smiled. "I'm not going to take advantage of you," he said.

"What's upstairs?"

"Perhaps the crumbs you need to follow as you take the next step in this journey you're on."

"What kind of crumbs?"

"Interesting ones, based on what you've just told me."

"So you do believe in signs?"

Chase smiled again, and his eyes sparkled. "Let me ask you a question," he said.

"Okay."

"Do you believe in God?"

Allie dropped her eyes, suddenly ashamed for reasons she couldn't quite explain. "I'm not sure," she said.

"That's honest," he said. "I respect that."

She stared at him, expecting judgment but saw none. "I take it you do," she said.

He nodded. "These 'signs' you just told me about—how else do you explain them?"

"Trey says they're a bunch of coincidences."

"A coincidence to one person is a miracle to another."

"So you have a better explanation?"

"Sounds to me like the Lord is trying to tell you something."

Allie shrugged, not sure what to believe. "But why now?" she asked. "If that's true, and I'm not at all certain it is, the timing couldn't be worse."

"Maybe the truth is that the timing couldn't be better but you just don't know it yet."

Allie saw no merit to that possibility.

"Come on," Chase said. "Let me show you what's upstairs."

"Will it lead me to my dad?"

"Only time will answer that."

Her curiosity overcoming her caution, Allie followed Chase as he led her to a large sunlit room facing the front of the house. A four-poster bed of ancient origin filled the room on one side. Intricate swirls of inlaid wood decorated the foot and head of the bed. A wooden washstand with a marble basin in the center stood by one side of the bed, and a nightstand with curved legs, small clawed feet, and more inlaid wood framed the other. A simple rectangular trunk—the plainest piece in the whole room—sat at the foot of the bed.

"This furniture is gorgeous," Allie said, admiring the craftsmanship of the pieces. "The pieces downstairs too."

"My grandfather made all of it," Chase said. "Everything in this house."

"Wow!"

"Yep, he was a carpenter, same as me."

"That explains the calluses on your hands."

"I earned every one of them."

"Are you as good as your grandfather?"

"No way, but I'm still learning. Maybe someday."

"Where's your workshop?"

"In the barn; I'll show you later if you have time."

Allie nodded, and Chase stepped to the trunk, pulled it open, and picked a picture album off the top of the stack of belongings that lay inside. "These have been here awhile," he said, handing her the album. "Have a seat and take a look."

Allie's hands trembled as she flipped it open and sat down on the edge of the bed. Chase took a spot a discrete distance from her. She eyed the pictures in the album, all of them carefully placed inside protective sheathing. Many of them contained images of her dad and Walt Mason when they were young—holding fish they'd caught, wearing baseball gloves, standing in front of all kinds of trucks, cars, and tractors.

"Before they went to Vietnam," Chase said, explaining the joyous look in both men's faces. "Not a care in the world."

"That changed," she said.

"For both of them."

66

"But my dad more than yours."

"I suppose so."

She flipped a page and saw another picture of her dad, this one not in a protective sheath. He stood posed in front of a house this time, the same house where she now sat on a bed. A child stood on either side of him, one of them a boy wearing a football uniform complete with pads, the other one none other than Allie herself, white gloves on her hands.

Allie picked up the picture, examined the boy for a moment, then glanced at Chase.

"It's you!" she said.

He laughed. "On my birthday," he said. "Eight years old."

"We knew each other?"

"Apparently so, although I didn't remember it until you called."

Allie brushed a hand through her hair, surprised at what she'd already discovered. She put the picture back, then opened another page of the book and sat up straighter. Another picture of her dad looked back at her; his eyes had noticeably changed. No longer did they sparkle with life and hope. They were now dark and somber, haunted and fearful.

"This is after the war," she said, as certain of it as anything she'd ever said.

"Yes, the date is on the back."

She took it out of the protective sheath and examined the date—May 1972, thirty-three years ago. "He was so young then," she said. "But look at his eyes; they look ancient. Like he's seen too much."

Allie fell quiet, her mind busy.

Then she said, "I have to find out what happened to him in Vietnam. That's the key to this."

"I know."

She flipped the page one more time. A last image stared back at her, and this one shocked her more than any of the others. It showed her dad again but much older now. He had gray hair, wrinkles at his mouth and eyes, a gaunt body, obviously wracked by the years and the despair he carried through them. He looked ill to her, like a man whose motor had pretty much run empty of fuel.

"When was this taken?" she asked.

"About a year ago, when he came through here."

She faced Chase, and tears welled in her eyes. "I don't understand," she said quietly. "He came this close to home but never drove to see me and Mom?"

Chase reached for her hand but then stopped, stood, and walked to the window. The sun shone on his back, and Allie stared at him and felt more alone than ever in her life. For several seconds she stayed quiet, her eyes moist.

"He did come to see you," Chase said.

"What?"

Chase shoved his hands in his pockets and faced her again. "I heard him and my dad talking," he explained. "Uncle Jack told Dad he needed to square a couple of things away—needed to check on his family."

"Before what?"

"He never said."

Allie pointed to the picture. "Was he sick?"

"He never said anything, but he sure looked it."

Allie tried to make sense of what she'd learned but found it more confusing. If her dad had come to see her and Gladys in the last year, why hadn't she seen him? Another thought poked at her. Had her mom seen him but denied her the opportunity?

"Are you sure he came to see us?" she asked Chase.

"I know he said he wanted to. What happened after that, I can't say. He left here for a couple of days, then returned for a few more, then left for good."

"Any idea where he went from here?" she asked.

"Yes."

Allie jumped up. "Where did he go?"

"He went to Vietnam," he said. "My dad too; they were gone close to a month."

Allie froze, trying to make sense of it. Her dad had come to Knoxville after years of absence and may or may not have come to visit her and her mom. After that he'd headed to Vietnam. But why? Vietnam had destroyed him. Why go back to such a nightmarish place?

"Why did they go to Vietnam?" she asked.

"I don't know. I never heard my dad say, and Uncle Jack never showed back up here."

Allie rubbed her eyes, then decided what she had to do next. "I need to talk to your dad," she said.

"If we can find him," Chase said.

"What time is it in Europe?"

"I don't know. Are they five hours ahead of us? Six?"

"I need to check."

"I'll have to reach my sister, see if she knows their exact location."

"Can you call her now?"

"Phone is downstairs."

Allie took a step back, and Chase moved past her and back down the stairs. She followed. In the kitchen he picked up a cell phone, pointed her to a chair at the table, then punched in a number. After waiting several seconds, he shook his head and punched the phone off.

"Voice mailbox," he said. "I was afraid of that; she's a high-powered lawyer for a firm in Knoxville. Might be hours before I can track her down."

"I don't have hours," Allie said.

"I don't know what else to do," Chase said.

Allie considered her options and realized one big one still remained unexplored. "Your folks' house," she said. "Wonder if we would find anything there to help us with this?"

Chase moved to the table and straddled a chair, his eyes wide. "You want me to go snooping around my parents' house?" he asked.

"Not snooping," she said. "You check their mail already; we'll just take a look around while you do that, see if we see anything interesting."

"What do you do for a living?"

"Teach and coach girls' basketball."

"Sound like a detective to me."

"I'm on a quest."

"You don't really expect to find something lying around on a table, do you?"

"Who knows?"

Chase arched an eyebrow. "Don't you need to get back home?"

"How far to your parents' house?"

"Thirty minutes tops."

"An hour and a half, then I'm headed back."

Chase lifted off his cap and studied the inside as if looking for the secret of life. "I don't know that I feel good about this," he offered.

Allie leaned forward, her eyes pleading. "I'm desperate," she said. "If I don't do this now, I know I never will. I'll get married and live the rest of my life without ever knowing what happened to my dad. Do you want that on your conscience?"

Chase shoved his hat back on, stared at her for several seconds, then smiled. His smile lit up the whole room. "In for a penny, in for a pound," he said.

"So you'll take me there?"

"What can I say? I'm a sucker for a pretty face, and you've certainly got one of those."

He hopped up, and she stood with him. A question she'd wanted to ask since she met him popped back into her head. "No wife?" she asked before she could stop herself.

"Do you see one anywhere?"

A slight thrill snapped through Allie, but she quickly pushed it back. A woman getting married in two weeks had no right feeling pleased that another man didn't have a spouse. A new question appeared. Why wasn't Chase Mason married?

"We'll take my truck," Chase said, interrupting her thoughts.

"I can drive."

"No reason for that; this is right on your way back. That is, unless you don't trust me."

Too grateful to even suggest such a thing, Allie quickly responded, "Your truck will be fine."

They headed out a couple of minutes later, Chase's dog in the back, his big teeth grinning into the wind as Chase piloted the truck onto the highway.

"What's your dog's name?" Allie asked.

"Buster," he said, donning a pair of sunglasses. "He's a stray, been with me about four years."

Silence fell for several minutes.

"You got a pet?" Chase asked.

"A cat named Patch. Also a stray, two years ago."

"I hate cats. They make me sneeze."

For some reason this bothered Allie, but she kept that to herself. They rounded a steep curve. "Thanks for doing this," Allie said.

"It violates all my ethics, you know," he said.

"You're teasing me."

He grinned again, and his white, straight teeth lit up the truck. He propped his left arm on the windowsill and let the wind blow through. He looked like a man without a care in the world.

Allie pointed to his hat. "You graduate from Tennessee?"

"Where else would a good Tennessee boy go?"

Allie smiled and spent the next few minutes pulling basic information out of him. He'd earned a business degree from the University of Tennessee and played football there for two years until a knee injury ended his career. He'd spent the last few years on the family farm, gradually developing a statewide reputation as a maker of custom furniture.

"It's a good living," he told her. "Quiet, steady, lets me use my hands, express a little bit of artistry, a whole lot of sweat."

"If you're anywhere near as good as your grandfather, it must be a whole lot of artistry," she said.

"I'm nowhere near his quality."

"I'm sure you're being modest."

"What about you?" he asked, changing the focus.

"Mars Hill College, got a teaching degree, played basketball there."

"An athlete."

"I'm tall, anyway; my coaches weren't always too sure of the athlete part."

"Now who's being modest?"

"Just truthful."

The road headed down a steep incline. "Isn't Mars Hill a Baptist school?" he asked.

"It's connected to Baptists, but I don't know how closely anymore."

"None of that ever stuck on you?"

"The religious part?"

"Yeah."

"Apparently not."

Allie sensed a slight disappointment in him and felt sad because of it. For some inexplicable reason, she wanted Chase to like her.

"I expect you're a good coach," he said.

"We've won our share of games—and one state championship when I was an assistant coach in Asheville."

"You ever have any girls go on to play in college?"

"Six."

"Wow."

"I'm proud of them."

They drove in silence for a while. The road curved, then rose and fell with the terrain; the sun warmed the truck; the blue sky beamed down on them. Allie rolled down her window and let the breeze blow through her hair. Chase eyed her for a split second, smiled slightly, then turned his gaze back to the highway. Allie felt at ease. Odd that riding with a man she'd met only a couple of hours ago seemed so natural.

"Why aren't you married?" she blurted, her mouth ahead of her good sense.

He glanced quickly at her again, then stared back at the road. "That's a pretty bold question," he said.

"Forgive me, but it just slipped out."

He chuckled. "You're not the first one to ask it."

"I guess not."

"My mom is after me all the time."

"So?"

He looked to her once more and scowled just a little. "It's personal," he said. "Leave it at that."

"Sorry."

"No problem."

Allie propped her elbow on the windowsill and stared out at the woods. The road rolled past, and silence fell again for several minutes. Worried that she'd upset him, Allie waited for Chase to speak again.

Finally, when he didn't seem inclined to do so, she faced him. "Why are you doing this for me?" she asked.

"I'm a helpful kind of guy," he said just a touch flippantly.

She considered the answer, recognizing it as the truth but also sensing more to it than that. "What else?" she asked.

Chase scratched an ear. "You won't believe me if I tell you," he said.

"Why don't you try me?"

"I don't know that I should . . . it might scare you."

"Any more than what I've told you about me scares you?"

"About the same, I suppose."

Allie squinted at him but didn't press.

After a couple more minutes, he slipped off his sunglasses, then said, "Two days before I heard your call on my folks' answering machine, I did some spring cleaning at my house, threw away a lot of junk from the cellar and attic. In the process I found that trunk I showed you a little bit ago; it was in the attic, covered up with a bunch of old bedspreads, blankets, quilts."

He paused as if Allie could guess the rest of the story, but she had no clue.

"So?" she said.

"So when I found that trunk, I opened it. I wanted to see what was inside."

"That's a normal thing to do."

"I dug through it, found that picture album."

"I still don't follow."

He chewed on the end of the sunglasses. "That picture of you and me," he said. "Did you notice that it was loose, unlike the others, and on the top of the page?"

"Yes."

"Did you wonder why it was loose?"

"Not really."

"There's a reason."

She waited for him to give it, but he didn't, so she pressed him. "I assume the reason is important?"

Without a word he pulled the truck into a small driveway on the side of the highway, put it in park, and faced her. Allie's heart revved up a notch.

"When I saw that picture, the one with me and you in it . . ."

"Yes?"

75

He shook his head. "You'll think I'm some kind of religious fanatic," he said softly.

"No," she said. "I won't."

He took off his cap and rubbed his hands through his hair. "You promise you won't laugh?"

"I promise."

He nodded. "Okay. When I saw you in that picture, something happened to me."

"You throw up or something?"

"This is serious."

"Okay, what happened?"

He swallowed hard. "If I didn't think it made me sound like a lunatic, I'd say God spoke to me."

In spite of her earlier assurances, Allie found it tough to keep a straight face. "You mean like an audible voice?"

"Not exactly; more of an impression in my heart, a sense of a message pushing at me."

Allie bit her lip. Given her recent experiences, she couldn't completely write off Chase's explanation, but she still rebelled against the notion that some higher being, even if one existed, cared enough about humans to actually speak to them, audible voices or not.

"And what do you think God said to you?" she asked, trying to stay focused. "Or impressed upon you?"

Chase dropped his eyes. "This is the weirdest part of all."

"We seem to be into weird today."

"God said you were the woman I was going to marry."

Allie pressed back against the seat, her head spinning. She wanted to jump out of the truck, run away from this man, hitch a ride back to her car, and head it straight back home. A tinge of fear hit, and she wondered what kind of man sat beside her barely an arm's length away. She started to speak, but Chase suddenly laughed, and that broke the tension. After a moment Allie laughed too. Chase shook from head to toe, his body wracked with the absurdity of his last statement.

"You should see your face!" he said. "I've . . . never . . . seen anybody so shocked."

Allie rocked back and forth with laughter.

"I told you it was weird," Chase howled, "but I didn't know how weird until I actually said it!"

Allie's sides hurt from laughing.

"You're going to be married in two weeks!" He chuckled, his laughter easing a little. "So I guess God got this one wrong."

"Or your hearing has gone bad."

"That may be it, as old as I'm getting."

"A Carolina girl can't marry a UT guy," she roared.

Chase grabbed his ribs and continued to chuckle. Gradually the laughter died, and Allie took a deep breath and finally found her voice.

"You told me you believed in God," she said. "I can't say I wasn't warned."

"I didn't say my name was Moses though."

"God speaks to you often, does he?"

"Only when a woman I haven't seen since I was a kid—and didn't remember I'd ever met—is about to call."

"Thank goodness it's not more often."

Chase eased the truck back into the road and headed it back up the highway. For the rest of the ride, they both kept quiet, Allie with a close eye on Chase, half in mock fear and half in silent wonder. Until a few days ago, the notion of God speaking to somebody would have surely given her the heebie-jeebies. But now, because of her dad's eyes staring at her from a picture, she didn't know exactly what to believe.

Chase pulled his truck into the driveway of his parents' house, checked the mailbox, then led Allie inside.

"What am I looking for?" he asked, putting the mail in his back pocket.

"Your guess is as good as mine. Pictures, letters, souvenirs, anything to tell us what they did in Vietnam."

"The first time or the second?"

"Either."

Chase headed down a hallway toward the master bedroom. "Start in their closet," he said. "Though I have to tell you again, I don't feel good about this."

"They'd probably let you do this if they were home."

"I just wish I could ask them first."

"Will you try to reach your sister again later?"

"For the woman I'm supposed to marry, absolutely."

Allie cut her eyes at him and wondered if he was serious but couldn't tell. They stepped into a square bedroom—bed straight ahead, typical dresser and chest of drawers on opposite walls, family pictures on the walls, two rectangular windows covered with blinds and drapes.

"Over here," Chase said, pointing to a closet.

He opened the door, and she stepped closer to look inside. An earthy scent drifted off Chase, a mix of manly aftershave and fresh wood. For a moment Allie lost her focus on finding anything in the closet. Chase's powerful body, smooth voice, and easy humor created a powerful presence, one that again made her wonder how in the world he'd managed to stay single. What character flaw did he have that kept him from marrying?

Chase stood on tiptoe and examined the boxes and clothes on the top shelf of the closet but found nothing. A bunch of shoe boxes sat on the floor, and he quickly searched through them but again with no result.

"Nothing here," he said, backing out. "Let's try the study."

Allie followed silently as he made his way to a small study to the left of the bedroom and began sorting through the drawers of the desk. None were locked, and Chase made quick work of the contents.

"Papers, bills, receipts, stationery, and computer manuals—that's all," he concluded. "Another dead end."

"Where does your mom keep old photos and things?" Allie asked.

"She's got a sewing room. There are a couple of file cabinets in there."

"Lead the way."

In the sewing room, they found a wall covered with bookshelves and one lined with metal filing cabinets. A bed sat against the far wall with a sewing machine and chair beside it. Chase immediately stepped to the cabinets, opened the one nearest him, and lifted a manila envelope from it.

"Bingo," he said as he flipped open the envelope and held up a handful of photos. "Looks like we struck the mother lode."

He dropped the envelope on the bed, stepped to the cabinets, hauled out several more folders of photos, and placed them beside the first one. Then he plopped onto the bed, poured all the photos out, and pointed Allie to a spot at the foot of the bed.

"It could take a while to go through all these," he said. "I could use a little help."

"I didn't want to be presumptuous, start thumbing through your family's things without permission," she said, perching on the spot he indicated.

"*Presumptuous* is a big word for a lady jock."

Allie smiled and began sorting through the photos with Chase. A couple of envelopes contained nothing but black and whites, images of Chase's folks when they were young, some of them with people Chase identified as his grandparents, now both deceased.

"You take after the men of the family," she said, studying one of the pictures. "All of you are built like anvils, only taller."

"You calling me chunky?" he asked, pretending to pout.

"You're not exactly a bean pole," she said.

He laughed, and she opened another couple of envelopes. They both contained image after image, color this time, of a girl growing from a baby to a girl, then a teenager, then a young woman.

"My sister Julie," Chase said. "Two years younger than me."

"She's pretty."

"She thinks so."

"Not as bulky as you."

"Is that another shot?"

"Not at all; just glad for her, that's all."

Chase chuckled.

"Your mom is really organized," Allie continued. "One person per envelope."

"What can I say?"

Allie looked at another photo of Julie with a blond man. "Is this Julie's husband?" she asked.

"John Router, a good guy. They've got three kids, all girls."

Allie desperately wanted to ask Chase about his singleness, but he flipped a picture at her before she dared. "I was handsome as a child, at least," he said, indicating the photo.

Allie held up the picture and smiled. Chase in a little suit, bow tie, and shiny black shoes. "How old were you?" she asked.

"I think eight," he said.

"Why so dressed up?"

"Going to church."

She handed back the photo. "Did you go often?" she asked.

"Every Sunday unless I had a bone sticking out or was throwing up."

"You still go?"

"Yeah, but I don't wear the bow tie."

Allie's eyes locked with his, and something in her ached to understand him. What made an obviously intelligent man who had nobody forcing him to attend religious services go to such events? "Why?" she asked.

"Why don't I wear the bow tie?"

"No. Why do you go to church?"

Chase opened the last envelope of photos but ignored her question.

Allie waited for a moment for an answer, but when none

81

came she focused on the photos again. "Who's this?" she asked, grabbing a picture of Chase with an attractive brunette woman.

"A former lady friend."

"What happened with her?"

Again Chase fell silent. Allie dropped the photo, searched through the rest lying on the bed, then stopped as Chase finished the ones he held.

"Nothing else here," he said, standing and looking through the filing cabinets one last time. "No pictures of my dad or yours—together or apart. I'm surprised."

Allie stood too, not sure what to do next. Chase started putting the pictures up, and she helped him. When they'd finished, he shoved his hands in his pockets and faced her.

"Look," he said, staring at his boots. "Let me be straight up here. I feel really odd right now. I had a wild experience with that picture of you." He looked at her, his eyes intense. "Then you show up out of the blue, and I have this strange sensation the instant I see you. I want to get to know you, would like nothing better than to tell you all about me, why I'm not married, what I believe about God. I'm not ashamed of anything—my convictions, my past relationships with women—but I'm usually a shy guy, so it doesn't come easy for me to talk about all that, especially not with a stranger who will disappear from my life as quickly as she entered it. So just leave the questions out, okay? I'll do what I can to help you find your dad, but that's as far as it should go, don't you think?"

"I didn't mean to upset you," Allie said.

He took off his cap, looked into it for a moment, then placed it back on. "It's okay," he said.

"I'm honestly curious about your faith; I'm interested right now. Not sure why, but I am."

Chase lightly touched her elbow, and a shot of energy ran through Allie's arm where he touched her.

"I'm a believer," he explained. "Go to church, read the Bible, the whole bit. But I'm not one of those people you see on television, somebody who wears their faith like a neon sign. I'll talk to people about it once I know them, but you . . . well, I expect I won't ever know you, so . . ."

"I don't want to make you uncomfortable," Allie said, trying to understand.

He took his hand away and smiled, and the tension broke. "Go to dinner with me and maybe I'll tell you more," he offered.

"You'd use your faith as a bargaining chip?"

"When you get to my age, you use whatever you have."

Allie laughed, then turned serious again. "I'm engaged, remember?"

"Yeah, but you can't blame a guy for trying, can you?"

She focused again on the purpose of her trip. "I need to get going," she said. "Anywhere else we need to search here?"

He bit his lip and thought a second. Then his eyes lit up. "The computer," he suggested. "Digital images, maybe email too."

Allie arched an eyebrow. "Good thought."

They quickly made their way to the study again, and Chase took a seat in the chair at the desk and turned on the computer. Allie stood over his shoulder as he did a quick search, brought up a "My Pictures" file, and clicked on it. To her dismay, he found no pictures in the file.

"Okay," he said, manipulating the computer mouse. "Let's try email."

"Won't you need a password?"

"We'll see."

"And isn't this private?"

He turned and looked at her like she'd burped without covering her mouth. "You're the one who got me into this. No time to get a conscience now."

She threw up her hands, palms out. Chase shook his head, faced the computer again, and clicked the email icon, and the program loaded without asking for a password.

"Let's check Mom's email first," he suggested. "Go back to last March, when Dad went to Vietnam with Uncle Jack. See if Dad contacted her during that time, from a hotel or maybe an airport."

"If she hasn't deleted them."

"She never throws anything away, probably doesn't delete much either."

Chase scrolled through his mom's emails until he reached the ones she received in March. "There we are," he said, clicking on an email. "Let's see what we've got."

The email appeared. "It's from Dad," Chase said.

Allie held her breath as she read the message.

> Beth, we're here. The computer hookup at the hotel seems to be working. I hope this reaches you. It was a long trip, hope it's worth it before it's over. Jack is tired, not looking well, but he won't tell me what's wrong. I'll tell you more later. Love, Walt.

Chase looked at Allie, and she pointed him back to the

email. He searched through several more until he found another one from his dad.

> Beth, we're almost to Dinh Tuong, close to where the worst of it happened. We should get there tomorrow, if the transportation we've arranged shows up. You never can tell over here, things don't always go like clockwork. I'm just glad this hotel had computer lines. I wonder if Jack is going to get through this, he seems sicker every day. Love, Walt.

Allie pulled up a chair from the corner and waited while Chase found a third email. This one was longer. Allie leaned forward as she read it.

> We just got back from Dinh Tuong. I'm worn out. Things have changed some but not as much as I imagined they would have. Jack didn't say much the whole time, just walked around, like stepping on hallowed ground. I wish he could get past what happened here. Funny how Vietnam affected the two of us so differently. I feel guilt too, you know that, but I managed to overcome most of it—at least most of the time. Jack, though, I don't know. He's carried his guilt like a truck on his back, and it's gotten heavier every year. Anyway, it's done. We visited the ghosts; I pray this trip will give him the strength to beat them, pray it's not too late for him. Talk to you again soon, maybe I can call when I get back to the airport. Love, Walt.

Allie wanted to cry but held it back. Chase clicked through the email folder and came to one more from Vietnam.

> Beth, we're headed out later today. But we got a shock this morning. A man from the village where we were

yesterday showed up at the hotel, said he had heard some Americans had come there and he wanted to talk to us. You won't believe what he said. The girl, the one I've told you about? The one he felt responsible for? The man said the girl and her mother made it out. He said they came to America. Can you believe it? Jack almost wouldn't let the man go. He kept him here for over an hour, pumping him for information. I don't know what Jack will do when we get home. I just want him to be healthy enough to find out what he can before it's too late. I'll tell you more when I get home. What a trip! Love, Walt.

Chase leaned back and locked his hands behind his head. Allie stared into her lap, her hands clenched.

"What does it all mean?" she asked softly.

"I'm as clueless as a two-year-old at a Mensa convention."

"It's the same question," she said. "What happened in Vietnam?"

"What caused all the guilt my dad talks about?"

"And who's the girl he mentioned, the one who came to America with her mother?"

"And what do the two of them have to do with our dads?"

Allie considered a horrible thought but then pushed it away. "Mysteries," she said. "One after another."

"You need to talk to my dad," he said.

"Yes I do, and to my mother."

"You think that's wise?"

"I'm not sure."

"You want copies of these?" he indicated the emails, and

she nodded. He quickly pulled them up, printed them out, and handed them to her.

"I feel a little guilty about this," she said.

"I'll repent for the both of us on Sunday."

She laughed, and he pulled his cell phone from his pocket and tried to reach his sister again but with no luck. "Sorry," he said, putting up the phone. "I'm sure I can reach her later if you want to wait, but . . ."

Allie looked at her watch and stood quickly. "I have to go," she said. "I'm already late."

He stood too, his hands in his pockets. "I'll talk to Julie soon as I can," he offered. "Call you with the number so you can reach my folks."

"It'll probably be too late to call them today," she said.

"Then you can try first thing in the morning."

"They'll think I'm a lunatic."

"I'll call them first and assure them that you are."

"Thanks a lot."

He smiled and headed through the house and back to the truck, Allie right behind him, the emails clutched tightly. They stayed quiet for the ride back to the farm, both of them lost in their own thoughts. When they reached the farm, both climbed out, and Allie hurried to her car. Chase leaned to the window as she started the engine, and she powered down the window.

"Will you be with your fiancé tonight?" he asked.

"Yes."

"Hope I don't make him jealous when I call you."

"He's very mature; I'm sure you won't."

He smiled for a moment, then became serious again. "I'll say a prayer for you, Allie Wilson, for good results for your quest."

"I'm sure it can't hurt."

He tipped his cap, and Allie rolled up the window and drove away, her last view of Chase that of a man posed in the yard, his hands shoved deeply into the pockets of his jeans. Although she loved Trey, something about Chase Mason made Allie look forward to his call, even if its purpose had nothing to do with anything romantic.

SECTION 4

My soul, her wings doth spread and heaven-ward flies,
The Almighty's mysteries to read in the large volume of
   the skies.

William Habington

6

After leaving a message on Trey's cell phone, Allie made her way straight to her mom's house. Before she did anything else, she needed to know one thing for certain. Did her dad come to see them after his trip to Vietnam? If so, why? Equally as important, why hadn't her mom told her about it?

All kinds of possibilities entered Allie's head as she drove up to Gladys's house, and all of them frustrated her, made her angry even.

First, Chase had it all wrong, and her dad never visited her mom.

Second, her dad came but didn't let her mom know it.

Third, he visited Gladys, but she didn't tell Allie because she wanted to protect her.

Fourth, her dad showed up, but he told Gladys not to tell her.

Allie warned herself to stay calm and give her mom a chance to explain. She found Gladys in the kitchen, a bunch of cut flowers on the countertop by the sink, a couple of clear vases nearby. Gladys wore a straw hat and held her hands under the water, washing them. Allie's temper softened as she saw the flowers—her mom loved beautiful things; how could she stay mad for long at a woman like that?

Gladys smiled as Allie stepped to her and kissed her on the cheek. "Glad you're back," Gladys said. "You find out anything interesting?"

Allie studied her mom, searching for a hint of deceit or evasion but saw none. "I met Chase Mason."

"I remember him as a handsome boy."

"Now he's a handsome man."

"You ought not say such things."

"I'm getting married, Mom, not going blind."

Gladys laughed and poured water into a vase, then put flowers in.

"Chase tell you anything about your dad?"

Although not wanting to cause any argument, Allie couldn't avoid asking the question that had burned in her since talking to Chase. "When did you last see Dad?" she blurted.

Gladys's hands stilled for an instant but then picked up another bunch of flowers. "Why do you ask?"

"Because Chase told me he saw Dad just about a year ago. He heard him and Mr. Mason talking. Dad told Walt he planned to come here, that he needed to get some things settled, like he had something big about to happen and wanted some loose ends tied up."

Gladys faced her now, her jaw set. "I don't see how bringing this up helps anybody," she stated. "Let bygones be bygones, that's my motto; it's the only way I've made it all these years. I've told you that more than once."

Allie stepped closer. "I need to know, Mom. Did Dad come through here or not?"

Gladys dropped her eyes, her head nodding. "About ten months ago."

"Why didn't you tell me?"

Gladys raised her head, and a fierce determination played on her face. "The same reason I never told you about any of the times he showed up. What good would it do? He never stayed more than a couple of days. The man drifted in and out faster than fog on a sunny day."

"But he's my father!"

"And I'm your mother, and a mother is supposed to protect her young. I've done that your whole life, and in my judgment it made no sense for you to see him; you'll have to trust me on that."

Allie ground her teeth to keep from crying. She felt trapped between her appreciation for all Gladys had done for her over the years and her anger at the decision she'd made without ever talking to her.

"But I'm grown-up now," she said. "I'm old enough to have made that decision for myself."

Gladys turned back to her flowers. "Jack always left it to me what to do about seeing you, and I didn't see the good in it. Until the last visit, he always showed up drinking, worse every time—more gaunt and haunted, less and less of his old self visible as the years passed."

"And this last time?"

Gladys filled a vase with water. "This last time he was sober."

"Then why didn't you let me see him?"

Gladys stopped, turned to Allie, and took her hands. "I don't claim to be a perfect mom," she said, "and maybe I made a mistake this last time, I don't know. But I did what I thought best for you. Please believe that."

Allie hugged her mom and let her tears flow. "I do believe that." She sobbed gently. "But I . . . I don't know . . . I have to see him before I'm married. Something in me is forcing me to search for him; I can't seem to get past that."

Gladys patted her back and let her cry it out. When she'd finished, Allie eased back and wiped her eyes.

"Did Dad give any indication where he was going from here?" she asked. "Where we might find him if we wanted?"

Gladys shook her head.

"You're telling me the truth?"

"Yes, sweetheart."

Allie wiped her eyes again. "It's a hard time, Mom."

"I know."

Allie helped Gladys finish the last of the flowers. "I need to ask you one more thing," she said as they placed them on the kitchen table.

Gladys pointed her to a seat, pulled out two glasses, filled them with orange juice from the refrigerator, handed one to Allie, and sat down beside her.

Allie sipped from the juice, then said, "Chase said Dad went to Vietnam after he came here. Any idea why he did that?"

Gladys shook her head.

"Did Dad ever say anything to you about a girl in Vietnam?"

"What kind of girl?"

"I'm not sure."

Gladys set her glass down. "What's this about, Allie? You trying to tell me your dad had a woman while he was in Vietnam?"

Allie hung her head, her mom's words expressing what she'd feared since she first read Walt Mason's email. She pulled the printed emails from her pocket and handed them to Gladys, who took them, slipped a pair of reading glasses from her shirt pocket, and set them on her nose.

Allie waited until Gladys had finished the emails, then asked, "So what do you think?"

Gladys read the emails once more, then took off her glasses and chewed on one of the stems. "I knew something happened in Vietnam, but Jack never told me what," she said soberly. "I encouraged him to talk about it, suggested it might help him if he poured it all out, but he never did. I think he wanted to protect me; that's the feeling I always got when anything came up."

Allie laid a hand over her mom's. "I don't think this is about another woman," she said. "That doesn't feel right somehow, no matter how it looks."

"A lot of soldiers took Vietnamese girls," Gladys said. "Your dad was no saint; he'd be the first to tell you that. If he had a woman in Vietnam, that would certainly explain all the guilt he felt."

Allie stared out the window. Was this the answer? The reason her dad left her and her mom? He fell in love with a Vietnamese woman? Brought back that guilt when he returned home? Started drinking to cover the guilt?

She took the emails from her mom and read through them once again, and a new, even more horrifying thought hit her. Had her dad had a child by a Vietnamese woman? The email spoke of a girl and her mother. Was the girl the woman with whom her dad fell in love? Or was the girl his daughter and the woman her mother? And what did the email mean when it said they'd come to America? Had they come years ago or just recently? Did Allie have a half sister living somewhere in the United States?

Allie dropped the emails on the table and hoped her mom's mind didn't run the same channels as hers. To believe that your husband had taken up with a woman during a war might hurt, but to believe he'd fathered a child would cut even deeper; it might destroy.

"I believe it's something else," Allie said, facing Gladys again. "I just know it is."

Gladys waved her off. "Let it go," she said. "It's water under the bridge either way."

Allie took a drink of juice, her heart churning. She tried to focus on matters at hand instead of speculating so much. "Chase is going to call me tonight," she said.

"Why?"

"He's calling his sister for a number so I can reach his dad."

"And you want to do that because . . . ?"

"The same reason I went to Knoxville."

"You're still trying to find Jack?"

"All this has made the search even more urgent."

Gladys started laughing, but Allie knew no mirth lay in it. "You beat all, child," Gladys said.

"I can't just give it up," Allie insisted.

"Sure you can; I did a long time ago."

"But why, Mom? Dad visited us less than a year ago. You said he wasn't drinking. I think he's trying to send me a message; maybe he wants me to know it's time for us to see each other again."

"I just don't think that's it," Gladys said.

"But how can you be so sure?"

"Just a feeling."

"Well, I have a feeling too."

"I believe my feeling trumps yours."

"Why?"

"Because my feeling tells me that the last time I saw Jack was the last time I ever would."

Although Allie knew she needed to go assist Trey at the house, she found it impossible to do. After collecting every picture of her and her dad that her mom possessed, Allie took them to her apartment and spent the rest of the afternoon trying to remember Jack Wilson. Trying to remember the day he took her to the fair, as one picture showed. Trying to remember the black puppy with the white circle around his left eye that a third image conveyed. Trying to remember her fourth birthday party, as another depicted—the last one with him home.

As she examined the pictures, it seemed that a bit of memory emerged every now and again, a sliver of recall here, another one there. She tried to enlarge the memories, expand the random sensations of what she thought she'd experienced, but she found it impossible. For the most part, her past with her dad remained a blank—nothing but fog and dark.

Allie lay on her bed with the pictures around her as the sun drifted through the afternoon sky, the window open to the sound of birds chirping, and wondered if this happened with all people, if the days of their childhood—especially the earliest days—always receded into the shadows and disappeared. Or was it just her? Had she washed out these memories of her dad, scrubbed them clean from her mind so she wouldn't have to deal with the truth of a father she no longer had, a father who had run away and left her and her mom high, dry, and alone? Is that what a little girl did to protect herself from the hurt of a father disappearing?

Why, Dad? she wondered. *Where are you now? Why am I so consumed by this now, of all times?*

Unable to answer her questions, Allie let the afternoon drift away. Weary from the mental strain of the past few days, she eventually closed her eyes and dozed. Dreams sifted through her slumber. Her dad in a jungle . . . a faceless Vietnamese woman . . . her dad standing at a distance, his body thin and emaciated, almost a ghost, his right hand pointing her way, the forefinger beckoning her toward him . . . his right arm waving her closer . . .

Allie saw herself as if looking down from the clouds . . . she wanted to go to her dad but couldn't . . . something held her back . . . some chain, shackles . . . she strained against the chains and almost broke free, but . . . a ringing called her back . . . a ringing . . . a ringing.

Allie woke to the sound of the phone on her nightstand. Jerking up, she grabbed the phone.

"Hello?"

"Where are you?"

"Trey . . . uh . . ." She rubbed her eyes to wake up as she recognized his voice. Dark had almost fallen outside.

"Your message said you were coming to the house," he said, his frustration obvious.

"What time is it?"

"Past seven."

"I'm really sorry . . . I went to Mom's when I got back from Knoxville, then here. I stretched out for a few minutes, fell asleep. Where are you?"

"At Toby's Ribs. I called your cell."

"I left it in the car."

Trey fell silent.

"I said I was sorry," Allie said, "but I was really tired."

"Not from helping me."

"Hey," Allie said, her regret now tinged by a touch of temper. "I apologize, okay. What else do you want?"

Trey took a big breath. "You coming to eat with me or what?"

"Yes, give me twenty minutes."

"I'll go ahead and order, if that's okay."

"Yeah, good."

She hung up and quickly refreshed her makeup, brushed her teeth, and combed her hair. Ten minutes later she pulled up in front of the local rib joint and rushed inside. Trey sat in the booth where they almost always sat, the one to the right and in the far back corner. Two glasses of water, silverware, and two salads decorated the table. Trey stood as she reached him.

"Sorry," she said again as she laid her purse on the table and took a seat.

Trey sat and waved her off. "It's okay now," he said. "I got frustrated. It's lonely in that house without you there." He reached for her, and she took his hands in hers.

Her cell phone buzzed. She glanced at her purse, wondering if the call was from Chase. It buzzed again. She looked at Trey. "I need to check the phone," she said.

"Let it wait," he pleaded. "You just got here."

The phone buzzed again, and she gently pulled her hands from Trey's, lifted the phone from the purse, and checked the number—a Knoxville area code.

She looked at Trey again; his mouth was tight with frustration. "I need to take this," she said.

"It's that important?"

"Yes." She clicked the phone and put it to her ear.

Shaking his head, Trey walked away toward the men's room.

"Hello?"

"It's Chase."

"Yes."

"You doing okay?"

"I'm at dinner with Trey. Did you talk to your sister?"

"Yes, finally. I have a number for you."

"I appreciate your doing this."

"Anything for the woman I'm supposed to marry."

Allie glanced toward the men's room, guilt eating at her, not because she'd taken Chase's call but because his words made her smile, something Trey hadn't done in a long time. "You have to stop saying things like that," she said.

"Is Trey listening?"

"No, not that it's any of your business. He's in the men's room."

"If you were my fiancée, I'd never let you talk to another man outside my presence."

"You're that jealous?"

"No, you're that beautiful."

Allie enjoyed the compliment a second but knew she needed to finish the call before Trey returned. "Just give me the number," she said.

"Okay."

She grabbed a pen from her purse and wrote the number on a napkin. Trey walked back up and took his seat across from her.

"Thanks for your help," she told Chase.

"You're going to call them?"

"First thing in the morning."

"I hope you reach them."

"Thanks."

"When will I see you again?"

"I don't expect you will."

Chase chuckled as if he knew some deeply humorous secret, then hung up. Allie ended the call, slid the phone back into her purse, and faced Trey.

"Was that the guy from Knoxville?"

"Yes. He gave me a number to reach his parents."

"I talked to Gladys; she said you were insistent on continuing this nonsense."

"You two are in agreement that it's nonsense?"

Trey dropped his eyes, but when he looked back up, they were still full of challenge. "Look," he said. "I'm a patient man, but this isn't the time for this. We have too much to do. Later maybe I'll even help you find your dad. But this has gone far enough, don't you think?"

The waiter showed up with plates full of ribs and potatoes and placed them on the table. Glad for the interruption, Allie tried to gather her thoughts. She knew the sensible thing to do, but right now that seemed impossible. How could she walk away from this quest, even for a little while? Would she take it back up again after her wedding? Or would she get so involved with life that she'd never return to it? And would it be too late even if she did? Something told her that time was important here, perhaps even crucial. Her intuition told her she couldn't afford to wait.

The waiter left, and Allie folded her hands in her lap and faced Trey.

"I asked you a question," he said.

Although she didn't like his tone, Allie tried to stay calm.

"I know all this is inconvenient," she said, "but it surprises me you don't want me to follow through with this until it hits a dead end."

"Why would I want that?"

She leaned closer. "Because you want me to be happy, and I don't believe I can be until I know what happened to my father. Isn't that a first principle of psychology—the need to connect with roots, origins, mothers and fathers?"

Trey rolled his eyes but then nodded. "You're right, of course," he said.

"I won't take any more time than absolutely necessary," she said. "And I'll be with you every moment I possibly can."

"What about the house?"

"You can take care of that."

"But Mother gave it to the two of us; she desperately wants us to move into it when we return from our honeymoon."

"If it's not ready, we can finish when we get back."

"That will greatly disappoint her."

"She'll get over it."

Trey arched an eyebrow, and Allie knew the look. "Sorry," she said, "but I can't govern my life by what pleases your mom. I want to make her happy, don't get me wrong on that, but I won't always be able to do so. You need to realize that now if you don't already."

"I'm all she's got," Trey said. "When we marry, we'll be all she's got."

Allie hesitated but then pressed forward. Might as well say what needed to be said. "I will do everything I can to honor your mother, but when we get married, I have to take first place in your life, not her. Are we clear on that?"

"We're clear," he said, his words even.

Although his words sounded right, his posture said otherwise. His hands squeezed his water glass, and his neck muscles were taut.

"You're angry with me again."

"Of course I'm not." He set his jaw as if clicking a steel trap into place.

Allie started to point that out to him but then decided to leave it alone. Perhaps it was best right now not to tell an angry psychologist that it might not be good for him to repress his anger.

7

After a fitful night, Allie woke at eight o'clock on Sunday morning, hurriedly showered, dressed, and picked up her phone. To her great surprise, she reached Walt Mason on the fifth ring. Her hands started trembling as she heard his voice.

"This is Allie Wilson, Jack's daughter," she began, wondering how he would respond.

Mason cleared his throat. "Your dad and I go back a long way," he said. "I hope you're doing all right."

"Yes, I'm about to get married."

"Wonderful."

Quiet fell for a moment, and Allie decided to push straight to the point. "I hate to bother you on your trip," she said. "But I need to ask you about my dad—when you saw him last, whether you know how I might reach him."

"I always wondered if you'd call someday."

"I suppose I should have done it sooner."

"Your mom give you my name?"

"Yes, I saw a picture of my folks with you and your wife. I asked Mom about it; that started it all."

"I'm sure it's been hard on you, the way he left and all."

"Not easy, but I never really had him in the first place."

"Your dad is a good man; you need to know that. He didn't leave you because he didn't love you."

"What do you mean?"

"He . . . how can I say it? . . . he feels too deeply."

"I don't understand."

"He's like an 'empath,' if I'm using the word right. Somebody who soaks up emotion from other people, takes it on his own soul. An 'empath' feels the weight of his problems plus the struggles of others too."

Allie combined this information with what the emails had told her and tried to make sense of it all but couldn't. "I don't see how that changes anything."

"Maybe it doesn't, but I just wanted you to know he loved you."

"Can you tell me where I might find him?"

Walt cleared his throat again. "I can't tell you that."

"Is it that you don't know or that you know and won't say?"

"A bit of both, I suppose."

"I don't understand."

"Look," Walt said. "Your dad moves around a lot, so I never know exactly where he is."

"But he stays in touch with you?"

"From time to time."

"Can you tell me where he was the last time he contacted you?"

"No."

Allie clenched the phone tighter. "Why not?"

"He swore me to secrecy."

Allie rubbed her eyes. This wasn't going well. "I don't get it."

"I don't like being in the middle like this."

"I'm sorry to put you in this position, but I need to find my dad, and I can't see any reason you shouldn't tell me what you know."

"I wish I could." He sighed. "But I can't. Your dad and I went through hell together; we're brothers in that. I can't tell you what I gave my word I wouldn't tell anybody."

Allie's heart sank, but then she tried another tactic. "Can you tell me what happened to him in Vietnam?" she asked.

Walt grunted. "No way."

"Same reason?"

"Even more so; a man doesn't revisit the worst moments of his life if he can possibly avoid it."

Allie bit her lip. Walt Mason was a stone wall. "I read your emails from Vietnam!" she blurted.

"What?"

"I made Chase find them, open them," she explained, not wanting to get Chase in trouble. "They talked about a girl, a woman. Who were they? I already know about them, so you aren't giving up anything by filling in a few blanks."

"You've got a lot of brass, young woman."

Allie knew she'd made him mad, but she didn't care. "I'm desperate here!" she exclaimed.

"Desperate doesn't give you permission to violate my privacy!"

Allie dialed back her frustration. "I'm sorry," she said. "I just feel like time is running out! My dad needs me, wants to talk to me!"

"He needs to tell you that face-to-face."

"But what if he can't? What if something's happened to him?"

"You're not getting a word out of me," Walt insisted. "Not after what you've done. And if you bother me again, I might just have you arrested when I get home."

Allie's heart sank as she realized she'd messed up. A man like Walt Mason couldn't be forced to do much of anything, and her efforts to shock him were the opposite of what she should have done. "I apologize again for reading your emails," she said.

"I blame that on Chase."

"I made him do it. I told you that."

"You must be a pretty woman; he's putty when that's the case."

Allie sensed a slight softening in Walt's voice. "Will you at least tell my dad I'm trying to reach him?"

Walt cleared his throat. "If he contacts me, I'll tell him you called."

"Thanks."

"You're welcome."

"Maybe I'll meet you and your wife someday."

"That would be fine."

Allie said good-bye, hung up, and leaned back on her bed. Although she knew it didn't make sense, she suddenly wanted to talk to Chase. She quickly dialed his number and got no answer but hung up without leaving a message. Strange, she thought, that she wanted to talk to Chase instead of Trey. But Trey cared nothing for any of this. Why should she want to talk with him about it?

Patch jumped up in her lap, and Allie scratched her behind the ears.

"What are we going to do today?" she asked the cat.

Patch seemed quite content to stay right where she was.

"What do you think Chase Mason is doing?" Allie asked.

Patch licked a paw.

Allie remembered it was Sunday and wondered if he was in church—maybe so, and without the bow tie. She remembered her last words to him last night, and the notion of never seeing him again felt completely wrong, more wrong than not going to assist Trey as he remodeled the home where they planned to spend the rest of their lives.

"I need to go help Trey," she told Patch. "He'll kill me if I don't; worse, his mom will kill me."

Patch purred, obviously not too bothered by the notion of Allie's ultimate demise.

For the next five days, Allie did exactly what everyone expected of her, and things fell back into a comfortable routine. She divided her hours between laboring on the house, taking care of wedding details, and spending time with her mom and Trey. To her relief, Trey seemed to have settled down again, and though she felt a little angry with him every now and again for the way he liked to control everything, she passed it off as normal for any woman in her thirties giving up her freedom for marriage. She thought of Chase from time to time—his easy laugh, his melodious voice, the woodsy smell of his cologne—but quickly pushed away the memories as inappropriate. A stranger looking at her through a telescope would have declared that all was normal.

Inside, though, Allie felt anything but peaceful. As she painted a wall at the house, she tried to figure a way to find her dad. As she stacked the finely wrapped wedding gifts pouring in from all over, she considered avenues to search for him. At night after she and Trey separated for the evening, she lay in bed and weighed her options.

As the days went by, she checked out—in her private moments—a number of avenues that occurred to her. She logged onto the computer and searched the Find a Friend and Locate a Relative websites, hoping against hope that entering her dad's name and date of birth might generate a lead or two. When that didn't pan out, she called directory information for every town within a hundred mile circle of Harper Springs and asked for a number for Jackson William Wilson. Again she had no luck. She even called the national Veteran's Administration—if her dad went to a VA hospital for medical help, maybe they would know where to locate him.

"We can't divulge any private medical information," said the government administrator she eventually reached.

"But I'm his daughter."

"The Medical Privacy Act," the administrator said. "Unless your father gives us written permission or you go to your state government and prove you're his immediate kin, my hands are tied."

"How long will that take?"

"It's the government, Ms. Wilson. Time is relative."

"More than a week?"

The administrator laughed.

"So I have to find my dad in order for him to give you permission to give me an address for me to find him, is that it?"

"Ironic, isn't it?"

Allie hung up and kept thinking, but by Friday evening, as she sat in her mom's kitchen right after dark with a chocolate chip cookie and a glass of milk before her, she knew she'd reached the end of her rope. No matter how much she hated it, she had to drop the hunt for her dad. She glanced at Gladys across the table and noticed a slump in her shoulders and dark shadows around her eyes.

"You all right?" she asked, forgetting her problems for a second.

Gladys shrugged, but Allie's antennae went up anyway. Although her mom stayed healthy most of the time, she occasionally fell into bleak periods when she became discouraged, even depressed. She'd even ended up in the hospital a couple of times in the past fifteen years, her doctor prescribing more rest and a series of antidepressants for a few months after each trip.

"Even a rock crumbles a little every now and again," the doctor had told Allie three years ago, the last time Gladys entered the hospital. "Your mom works hard. She needs to take better care of herself."

"You've been going at it too hard," Allie told Gladys. "You should take more time to rest."

Gladys waved her off. "I'm good," she said. "You know me, stout as a mule."

Allie dipped a cookie in milk and handed it to her mom. "I know you are for everyone but yourself. You'd rather walk on broken glass than admit you need some time off."

"It's a good thing you're getting married in a week," Gladys said with a hint of a smile as she nibbled the cookie. "Otherwise, I'd need to spank you for your smart-aleck mouth."

Allie smiled too but realized she needed to keep an eye on her mom over the next few days. An episode now would be disastrous for everybody.

Gladys placed the rest of the cookie on a napkin. "I'm going to miss you, that's all it is."

"I'm not going anywhere," Allie said. "Trey and I will live ten minutes away."

Gladys patted her forearm. "I know," she said, "but you'll be married. That changes things."

"Not between you and me."

"I hope not."

Allie's phone buzzed on the counter behind her.

"Must be Trey," Gladys said.

"You want to go to dinner with us?"

The phone buzzed again, and Gladys shook her head and pointed Allie to her phone. Allie stood and grabbed it. To her surprise, it wasn't Trey on the other end.

"Walt Mason here."

Allie walked onto the deck, shutting the door behind her. "You're home from Europe?" she asked.

"Got in about four hours ago."

"I assume you're not calling to tell me about your trip."

"You assume right."

Allie hesitated as Walt cleared his throat. "You need to come to Knoxville," he said.

"I can't do that," she said quickly. "I'm a week from my wedding."

"You want to find your father, don't you?"

"Of course I do, but . . ." Allie turned and looked through the window at her mom, still at the table, a cookie in hand. "It's complicated."

"That it is."

Allie walked to the deck's edge and tried to get a grip on her emotions. "I don't understand," she told Walt. "Just a few days ago, you wouldn't tell me a thing. Now all of a sudden you want me to drive to Knoxville?"

"Just come," he insisted. "You won't be sorry, I assure you."

Allie thought of Trey and knew his anger would boil over if she disappeared again so close to the wedding. "If you have something to tell me, just say it," she insisted. "I don't have time for another trip!"

"I won't tell you anything over the phone; it's too . . . personal."

"But why now?" she pressed. "What's different today from Sunday?"

"I found a letter when I returned today," Walt said. "From your dad."

"A letter?"

"Yes."

"What's in the letter?"

"The reason I called you."

Allie pressed again. "What's in the letter?"

"Just come to Knoxville."

"Why?" she shrieked.

"Because I don't have to keep my word to your dad anymore."

"Why not?"

"Because I think he may be dead."

SECTION 5

It is not the person with closed eyes who makes the discovery but the person with open eyes lucid enough to fit pieces together.

Michael Leiris

8

Allie left Harper Springs without telling Gladys exactly what Walt Mason had said, reporting to her only that she'd see her in the morning. From her mom's house, she drove straight to Knoxville, calling Trey on the way to inform him that she wouldn't be joining him for dinner. His icy tone told her all she needed to know about his feelings regarding her sudden trip, and he backed up the chill in his voice with an even colder one in his words.

"I could get suspicious here," he said.

"Of what?"

"You and Chase Mason."

"Don't be silly. I've met the man once."

"Your mom told me you said he was handsome."

"You and Mom have talked about that, have you?"

"We talk, yes. You know that."

Allie made a mental note to ask her mom to hold her tongue on a few things. "You know this isn't about Chase Mason," she told Trey, and she filled him in on what Walt Mason had told her.

"I asked you to leave this alone until after the wedding," he reminded her.

"Obviously, I can't do that."

"Tell me why again."

"Mr. Mason said my dad might be dead."

"If so, there's nothing you can do; even more reason to stop picking at this."

"But what if he's not?"

"But Mr. Mason thinks he is."

"But he doesn't know."

"You're really frustrating me with this. You know that, don't you? And Mom is completely confused, can't fathom for a moment why you're not at the house every day taking care of things."

Allie bit her lip to keep from spouting what she wanted to say. "I have to do this. You should explain that to her."

An awkward silence passed between them. Allie wondered why it felt so hard to talk to him lately. Fear suddenly ran through her, fear that if she kept going, something might forever change between her and Trey. Yet she knew she couldn't turn back.

"I'll call you on the way back," she said, her emotions blocking any other words.

"Yes, do that."

"Trey?"

"Yes."

"Do you ever say prayers?"

"What kind of question is that?"

Allie hesitated, not sure how to express her feelings. "I don't know," she said. "But I . . . I think something is happening here . . . to me . . . maybe my dad . . . perhaps to us. I need strength, more than I can find within myself. Prayers can't hurt, can they?"

"Delusion," he said. "That's all prayers are—empty words to empty air."

"Is that what you really believe?"

"It's what any sane person really believes."

For some reason Allie wanted to cry, but she didn't allow herself the luxury. "I'll call you later," she said.

"No matter the hour."

She pressed "end" and dropped the phone on the seat. Then, without quite knowing why, she rolled down her window, let the night air blow through her hair, and breathed a silent thought into the night sky. *Show me, God. Whatever it is I'm supposed to see, show me.*

The wind blew into her black eyes, and she drove on toward Knoxville, toward the man who knew more than she'd ever known about her father.

To Allie's surprise, she found Chase waiting for her on the front steps of his folks' house, his hands in his jeans pockets, his hair free from a baseball cap this time, his biceps bulging through a short-sleeved gold golf shirt. He jumped up as he saw her turn in the driveway and met her as she climbed out of the car.

"My dad called," he explained. "Told me you were coming. I hope you don't mind me showing up; thought it might help if I introduced you to Mom and Dad."

"Thanks," she said, secretly glad to see him again. "This is a little awkward."

"They're looking forward to meeting you," he said.

"You didn't tell them anything about your wild notion about us, did you?" Allie asked.

"No way! I keep my dreams to myself."

She nodded, and he led her through the front door. Walt and Beth Mason met them in the den, Beth with a tray in hand, tea and water on it. Allie took a glass of water as Chase introduced everyone, and Walt led them all to a seat.

"I'm sorry to bother you the night you get back from your trip," Allie started.

"I called you," Walt said. "Not your place to apologize."

Allie sipped her water while Beth disappeared into the kitchen with the tray.

Walt cleared his throat. Chase sat in a rocking chair, his hands clutching a tea glass in his lap.

"Might as well get to it," Walt said, pulling a letter from his pocket and handing it to Allie. "Here's the letter from your dad."

Allie set her glass on the floor and took the letter with trembling hands.

"No return address," Walt said. "And the postmark shows it was mailed almost three weeks ago from Asheville, North Carolina."

Allie opened the envelope and studied the handwriting on the one-page note. Scraggly, weak, obviously the writing of a tired, sick man. The words did nothing to dispel the impression of the writing.

Walt,

Hope you're well. Not too sure of that myself. I'm told by the doctors I've got some heart problems, some kind of strange condition with a funny name. I figure I might need a hospital. Probably never leave it once I get there.

I'm sending this so you'll get word to Gladys for me. Tell her I love her and Allie. Tell her I asked for their forgiveness.

Here's a key to a safety deposit box—Main Street Bank in Asheville. Not much in there. A few pictures, my dog tags, odds and ends, a couple of thousand dollars. Give it to Gladys for me.

I guess that's it for now. If I get better, I'll come see you this summer. If not . . .

Semper Fi,

Jack

Allie looked up, tears streaming, the key from the letter in her hand. Chase eased his rocking chair closer.

"He's dead," Allie sobbed.

"Not necessarily," Chase said. "The letter isn't clear on that."

"But it's probable, right? It's been three weeks since this was sent."

"We'll need to see; maybe he got better in those three weeks."

Allie shook her head. "I can't believe it," she cried. "It doesn't make sense. I go through this whole thing . . . this nutty search . . . for nothing? For him to turn up dead?"

Chase touched her hand, then pulled away. "I'm sorry," he said.

"We don't know if it's for nothing or not," Walt insisted.

"Maybe he's still alive and this letter is a clue to finding him."

"Or maybe not."

Chase leaned closer. "Even if he's . . . dead . . . that doesn't mean all this was for nothing. Maybe there's more here than meets the eye, some purpose in this we can't see."

"If he's not alive, I don't see how there's any purpose in it," Allie argued.

Chase held his hands out, palms up in resignation.

Allie wiped her eyes, her hopes dashed. "This is the end of it." She sighed. "Nothing else to do."

"Not necessarily," Chase said. "Dad and I have talked. He's going to contact the folks at the VA; if Jack went to a government hospital, somebody will know something."

"I already tried that," Allie said. "They won't tell you a thing."

Walt coughed. "I'm a veteran," he said. "Stayed in the Marines eight more years after Vietnam; I know some folks in the Pentagon. I'll make a few calls, maybe even fly up to Washington, see what I can find out."

"You'd do that for me?"

"Of course I will. It won't necessarily turn up anything, but it's worth a try."

"And you and I are going to Asheville in the morning," Chase said. "To take a look at this safety deposit box. Maybe your dad left something there that will tell us where he is."

"Or was."

"Yes, perhaps so, but until we know that for a fact, let's keep hoping."

Allie wiped her eyes and tried to think clearly. Did she dare drive to Asheville in the morning? Leave Trey again? What would he say? Did it matter? If he responded poorly, would she tell Chase she couldn't go? She could, of course, tell Chase to check the box without her. But she didn't want that, not really. Whether her dad was alive or not, she wanted to see the few belongings he had left behind. Those little items might be the only tangible part of him she would ever touch. It didn't seem right that someone else, even someone as close to her dad as Chase, would be the one to find those last slivers of his life.

Allie thought of Gladys and wondered what to tell her. Should she call her right now and inform her of what she'd learned? But how would that hit her in her frazzled state, already near the edge of her emotional and physical capacity?

No, Allie decided. She'd wait until she knew more before telling her mom anything. If her dad was dead, Gladys would learn soon enough. Until then, there was no reason to upset her.

Allie locked eyes with Chase. "Can you meet me at the bank in Asheville about ten in the morning?"

"You could spend the night here, and we could drive over together," Chase suggested.

"Do you want Trey to break the engagement the week before my wedding?"

"You want my honest answer?"

"No!"

Chase and Walt chuckled lightly. "Forgive him," Walt said. "He's smitten with you."

"I keep forgetting that you're spoken for," Chase said.

"You have a selective memory," Allie said.

"Women make him crazy," Walt said.

In spite of the circumstances, Allie felt a small thrill. "All women?" she asked.

"Now that you mention it, just two," Walt said.

"Two?"

"You and one other."

Allie stared at Chase. "What's her name?" she asked.

Chase dropped his head. "Now is not the time," he said.

"I know what you mean." Allie turned her thoughts back to the safety deposit box. "You think the bank is open to-morrow?" she asked.

"From nine to noon, I already checked."

"See you then."

When Allie called Trey the next morning, the conversation quickly became a disaster. "You didn't call me last night," he accused immediately.

"It was so late."

"I worried about you, could barely sleep."

"I had a lot to think about."

"Like what?"

Allie quickly detailed what had happened the previous night, reminding him to say nothing to her mom until she knew more. "I'm going to Asheville now," she said.

"You're doing what?"

Standing on her deck with the sun warming her face, Allie rubbed her forehead. "I have to do this," she explained. "A couple of hours tops. I'm back by lunch, and that will be the end of it."

"I don't know why it can't wait!"

"Because if my dad is still alive, this may lead me to him!"

"If that's the case, you can find him after we get back

from the honeymoon. If he's dead . . . well, it surely won't matter then."

Allie tried to take a breath. Was Trey right? Should she leave things alone for now? Logically, his way made the most sense. But she'd tossed logic out the window the second she decided to hunt for her dad. So why revert to it now? She was acting on intuition, instinct, gut feeling, mystery wrapped in riddles clothed in enigmas. She closed her eyes, listened to the chirping of a bird, tried to hear her heart, listen to her soul. A bee buzzed near her face, and she smelled the sweet scent of flowers blooming. *What?* she wondered. *Which way do I go?*

She opened her eyes. "I'll be back by lunch," she told Trey.

"I can't talk you out of it?"

"No."

"This really hacks me."

"I know."

"Is the Chase fellow going with you?"

Allie hesitated.

"He is, isn't he?"

"I wanted to ask you to come with me but knew you wouldn't."

"You're right about that; somebody has to be the responsible one around here."

She grabbed the deck rail and squeezed it. "I'm sorry this upsets you," she said.

"Sorry needs actions to back it up."

"I'll see you by lunch."

"We need to have a long talk when you return."

"Chase Mason is a friend, that's all," she insisted.

"I assure you, he won't be the subject of our talk."

Allie clenched the rail tighter, rebelling against the patronizing tone in Trey's voice. "I'll see you later."

She hung up and thirty minutes later piloted her car out of Harper Springs and toward Asheville.

Chase met Allie at the front entrance of the bank, a stately four-columned, red-brick building near the end of Asheville's central street. He wore khakis, a blue button-down shirt, and black loafers without socks.

"You look almost corporate," she said.

"I'm an educated man," he retorted. "I can look like a frat boy when I want."

She smiled, and they walked together into the bank. Inside she pulled the safety deposit box key from her purse and held it up. "Number 1868," she said. "Which way do we go?"

Chase quickly moved to a bank teller, talked a moment, then returned to her. "This way." He pointed. "Down the stairs one floor, then left."

A couple of minutes later, they reached the safety deposit boxes. Allie held up the key, and a bank employee waved them through a roped-off area. Chase touched her arm, and she halted.

"You want to do this by yourself?" he asked.

She immediately shook her head. "No, you come with me."

"Okay."

They moved into the roped area, and Allie found 1868 and stopped before it, key in hand. "I'm nervous," she said.

"I expect so."

She held up the key. "It's been worth it, no matter what happens."

"I think that's a good way to look at it."

She inserted the key and turned the lock. The box clicked, and she pulled it open, stepped to a small table, and set it down. Chase quietly followed. Allie peered inside. A large manila envelope stared back at her, and she pulled it out, opened it, and poured the contents onto the table.

Two small wads of cash lay before them, and she pushed the money aside without bothering to count it.

She found her dad's dog tags next. Her fingers touched them as if she were holding diamonds. "He wore these in Vietnam," she said, holding them so Chase could see.

Chase lightly touched her shoulder, then pulled his hand away.

Allie turned again to the envelope's contents—her dad's honorable discharge papers from the Marines, then a smaller envelope under that. Allie picked it up and showed it to Chase.

"This is it," she whispered weakly. "Whatever I'm supposed to find is in here, I just know it."

Chase moved closer. She could feel his breath on her neck, could smell the woodsy smell that seemed as much a part of him as his deep voice. Fighting her thoughts of Chase, she tore open the seal on the envelope and spilled out the contents.

Pictures again—at least ten.

But of whom?

Allie picked up the top photo—a color shot of her dad standing in front of a bar somewhere, a guitar in his hands, his hair long and wavy. She studied the image and wanted to know its history but knew she might never have the opportunity to do so.

She laid it down and looked through several more of

a similar kind. Her dad here and there, gradually getting older as the years passed, other people—strangers all of them—in some of them, her dad alone in others.

Allie's hands stilled as she reached another picture. A willowy Vietnamese woman—quite attractive—stood by her dad, he in his military uniform. A little girl stood by the two of them, her face showing unmistakable signs of both Vietnamese and American parentage. The girl's eyes were as dark as Allie's and seemed to stare out from the page, much like her dad's had when she found his picture two weeks ago.

Allie's eyes watered, and the picture blurred. She handed it to Chase, then hurriedly looked through the last three pictures in the envelope—two of them of her dad alone, the last one showing Allie with her mom and dad. She looked about the same age as the Vietnamese girl, and her eyes seemed just as dark, only not as intense.

Allie faced Chase. He opened his arms in sympathy, and she sagged into them and sobbed.

"I didn't want to believe it," she cried softly. "But . . . I can't . . . can't deny it any longer. Dad had a Vietnamese wife and daughter."

"There may be other explanations," Chase offered.

"But what? How?"

"I don't know."

Allie's tears stained Chase's blue shirt.

"I've got a half sister," she moaned. "That's what happened in Vietnam. That's the source of dad's guilt. That's why he couldn't stay with me and mom."

"I'm sorry," Chase said. "I'm sorry."

Allie leaned into his strength and thought of Trey. She wondered how he would have responded to this and wished she could say for sure that he would have been as sensitive as Chase. Although he was a psychologist, a man skilled in helping others deal with their emotions, Trey often seemed unable to face his own. Was he a doctor who couldn't heal himself? Or was she the problem, too spontaneous for his rigidity, too intuitive for his science, too something for his something?

She suddenly felt afraid, unsure of the future, and that scared her so much that she started to sob again. Chase didn't move, didn't do anything to take advantage of her, just stood like a rock and let her lean on him.

Allie thought of Gladys and tried to figure out how to report this to her. Indeed, she wondered whether she ought to tell her at all. Gradually, her tears subsided, and she leaned away from Chase and wiped her face.

"I'm a mess," she said.

"A little smeared mascara but not too bad."

She patted him on the shoulder. "You've been so kind," she said.

"That's me, kind man."

"What am I going to do?" she asked, pointing to the picture in his hand. "What do I say to my mom?"

"It's up to you," he said.

"Do I keep looking for my dad? Try to find this Vietnamese woman?"

"Whatever you want."

"But where do I start and when?"

"Not for me to say."

"You're a big help."

"I'm a kind man, not a controlling one."

Allie smiled slightly at the irony, then reached for the picture. As Chase handed it over, she caught a glimpse of the back and saw something written on it. She flipped it over.

555-888-4615.

"A phone number," she said, holding it up for Chase to see.

"Unbelievable."

"You think it can be that simple?"

"Only one way to find out."

"My cell is in my car."

"If that's what you want to do."

"Where's that area code?"

"Not sure."

"What will Trey think if I do this?"

"I don't think it should be up to him what you do."

"Or Mom?"

"She'll support you, I'm sure."

"She's fragile right now, and this could upset her. Maybe I need to think about this, what kind of Pandora's box I might open if I call this number."

"Whatever you decide, I'll help you if you want."

Allie flipped the picture over and studied it again for several seconds, then shoved everything but the photo back into the big envelope, put the box back up, and led Chase out of the bank and back to her car.

After thanking Chase again, Allie left him and drove straight back to Harper Springs, her mind a swirl of confusion. Although she didn't call the number on the picture, she did call information to ask about the area code. The operator told her it came from Missouri and the exchange sounded like St. Louis.

Reaching Harper Springs right after noon, Allie headed straight to Trey and found him sitting on a sawhorse in the kitchen. His khaki shirt was covered with paint, and his face was perspiring from his labors. A glass of tea and a ham sandwich sat before him on a workbench. Allie stepped to him, gave him a quick hug, and placed the picture on the bench.

"What's this?" he asked, examining the picture.

"You tell me," she said.

"Looks like your dad kept more secrets than anyone knew."

Allie's heart fell. She'd hoped Trey might come up with some other explanation for the photo. "Check the back," she said.

He turned it over and saw the phone number. "What's your next move?" he asked.

"I'm trying to decide whether to call the number or not."

"Interesting," he said, rubbing his chin.

"What should I do?" she asked.

He tossed the picture onto the bench. "You should leave your father where he obviously wanted to be left . . . out of your life."

She grabbed the picture and blew dust off it. "That's your best advice . . . as a psychologist?"

He took her hand. "No, it's my best advice as a fiancé. We're a week away, or have you forgotten that while you traipsed around the mountains with Chase Mason?"

Allie pulled away, her face red with increasing anger. "You're missing the point!" she argued. "Chase is a friend; I've told you that. He's helping me do something I want to do, something I would expect from you but haven't gotten!"

"So now I'm coming up short in comparison to Mr. Mason?"

"No . . . yes . . . look, Trey, you've had trouble with this from the start. I know that, but it's something I can't run from."

"If you were a counseling client, I'd call you obsessed," he said. "And that's never a good thing."

"Not even if it leads to a good end?"

"It never does. That's just the problem."

He picked up his tea glass and sipped from it. "You're going to call that number, aren't you?" he asked.

"I don't see how I can refuse."

"Even if I forbid it?"

Allie bit her lip to keep from lashing out. When she finally did speak, she kept her tone as even as possible. "I'm not a child," she said, "and I won't be treated like one."

"Suit yourself."

Allie started to step to him to push his hair out of his eyes and ease away from the precipice she felt they stood on, a precipice that led to an abyss she didn't want to fall into, but Trey interrupted her before she could move.

"You mentioned a few days ago that this would make you happy," he said. "But what about my happiness?"

Allie straightened, surprised that he wanted to turn the focus to him. "I don't see how any of this hurts your happiness," she said.

"You know I want the house finished before the wedding."

"Yes."

"And I want us to do it together."

"Yes."

"And I don't want you running all over the country with some strange man."

"I understand that."

"Then why aren't you complying with anything I want?"

"I've told you why . . . I can't escape this, whatever it is . . . that's the only explanation I have."

He grinned sarcastically. "Yes, the song, the dreams, the message from on high regarding the eyes, oh, the mysterious eyes. How can we deny them? It's practically equivalent to the angels telling Mary she'd give birth to the Son of God."

"You're mocking me."

"What do you expect?" He threw the tea glass to the floor, and it broke into a thousand pieces. "It's totally irrational, a side of you I've never seen. If you came to my office with this story and then acted the way you have the last two weeks, I'd be hard pressed not to advise hospitalization and medication."

"You don't mean that."

He stared at the floor. "Maybe not, but listen . . ." He gazed up at her, his eyes confused. "You're a sensible woman. Why this sudden leap into religious mumbo jumbo?"

"I told you I can't explain it."

Trey wiped his forehead with a pocket handkerchief. "Will you go find this woman if you reach her?" he asked, pointing at the picture.

"I haven't decided."

Trey glanced at his boots. "Yes, you have," he said. "No reason to lie to yourself . . . or to me."

Allie realized he'd read her correctly. "I have to do this," she said.

"We all have to do what we all have to do."

"What does that mean?"

"Make your call. Let me know what you find out. Then we'll see what I mean."

"Is that a threat?"

Trey looked her dead in the eye. "I will not be made a fool of," he said.

"That's not what I'm doing."

He waved her off. "Go on. I'll be here when you want to talk."

"I don't want my mom knowing about this just yet," she warned. "No reason to bother her until I know more."

Trey shrugged but didn't speak.

Once again Allie wanted to go to him, but he picked up a sanding machine and switched it on. Seeing no other option, Allie pivoted, left the house, and drove home. No matter what Trey did, she had no choice but to make the call to St. Louis. After that who knew what would happen?

SECTION 6

Every parting gives a foretaste of death, every reunion a hint of the resurrection.

Arthur Schopenhauer

9

Allie spent the day between her apartment and her mom's house, cleaning things out, throwing things away, making phone calls to her bridesmaids, who were scheduled to fly in on Thursday, stacking more presents as they arrived. Try as she might, though, she couldn't keep her mind off the St. Louis phone number. Although she now had it memorized, she still hadn't called it when the sun dropped. For some reason she didn't want to be alone when she made the call. What if the woman was her dad's Vietnamese mistress, the girl her half sister? She didn't want to hear that kind of news by herself. But who did she want with her?

Not her mom in her frail state. Besides, she hadn't even told her about the number yet.

Not Trey either—he'd shown he wanted no part of this.

She had a lot of girlfriends she could call. But how do you explain a circumstance like this to a girlfriend?

She rejected the idea and thought of one other person.

Chase. He was the one to be with her. But that felt wrong. In spite of her troubles with Trey, he was still her fiancé and in less than a week, her husband. What kind of woman would flee to another man at such a crucial time? To make it worse, if she went to Chase, he might wrongly interpret it, and she didn't want that.

More confused by the minute, Allie went to bed right at nine. Sadly, though, sleep wouldn't come. After an hour of tossing and turning, she got up and tried to call Trey but got no response, so she called Gladys.

"Hey," her mom said. "What's up?"

"I can't sleep."

"I know the feeling. You're less than a week away now, an exciting time."

"That's not it," Allie said.

"What then?"

"Me and Trey. We had a fight. I'm not sure what he's thinking right now."

Gladys took a breath. "A fight before a wedding is normal; don't worry about it."

"I'm afraid it's more than that. He's mad that I've tried to find Dad, thinks I've lost a screw or two."

"He's jealous, that's all."

"Of what?"

"Your time, your focus. He's caught up in preparing for the wedding, finishing the house. He wants you to feel as passionate about it as he does, and when he sees you distracted, it makes him think you're not."

Allie chewed at a nail. "I'm not sure I am," she admitted.

"How so?"

"I don't know . . . Trey seems so controlling lately, condescending, like he knows everything. If he's this bad before we get married, how's he going to be once I'm his wife?"

Gladys hesitated, and Allie kept going. "I don't know,

Mom, it's so scary right now. I'm . . . wondering about some things."

"Not your marriage to Trey?" Her mom sounded panicked.

"I don't think so, but . . . this has me thinking about other things, bigger things."

"What's bigger than a marriage?"

"God, maybe?"

"God?"

Allie chuckled at the notion she'd rolled out, how funny it must sound to Gladys. "Forget it," she said. "Maybe I do have a screw loose."

"You're nervous, that's all."

"You're right. Look, I'll call you tomorrow."

Allie hung up and fell back into bed.

She tried Trey's number again but didn't reach him. Probably at his mom's, Allie figured. At his mother's request, Trey kept his cell phone off when he visited her. She wanted his total attention, she told him, no interruptions from a phone.

Her cell phone in hand, Allie shuffled to her deck and looked up at the stars. Then, before she could stop herself, she called Chase. He answered immediately, almost as if waiting for her call.

"You still up?" she asked.

"It's just ten fifteen; I'm not eighty. Any news?"

"Nope. I haven't called St. Louis yet."

"Scared?"

"Yes. I don't want to be alone when I call."

"Trey's not into it, is he?"

"Nope."

"And you don't want to upset your mom."

"You're such a wise man."

137

"I'm wise and kind; what more can you want?"

"Humble would be good."

Chase chuckled. "You want me to be with you when you call?"

Allie leaned over the deck. Although she'd called for just this reason, hearing it said frightened her. It moved their friendship to a new level, and she didn't know how to handle that.

"I'm not sure," she said. "I figured I'd never see you again. Wedding next Saturday, you know."

"I don't mean to press, but you know I'm your friend."

"You won't try to take advantage of me in my vulnerable state?" she asked, half teasing.

"I'll be a perfect gentleman. As long as you're engaged, I'm a friend, nothing more."

"I need a friend right now."

"I can be there in an hour and a half."

"Is that too late to call St. Louis?"

"They're an hour behind us. I can be there by eleven forty-five, ten forty-five their time. That should be okay—in an emergency, anyway."

Allie quickly gave him directions to her place. "Chase," she said.

"Yes?"

"Park in the back, okay?"

"I read you loud and clear."

She hung up and studied the stars again. What in the world was she doing? Although not sure, one thing was certain. She trusted Chase. If he said he'd be her friend, she could count on that. She retreated to her bedroom and began to dress, her heart thumping with a combination of fear, guilt, and excitement.

Chase arrived at just past eleven thirty, and Allie opened the door before he reached it. She quickly waved him inside, glanced around to make sure no one had seen him, and shut the door.

"You're acting like a criminal in a hideout," he said as she turned to him.

"I feel weird," she said. "Maybe you shouldn't be here."

"I'll leave if you want."

She shook her head. "No, you're here. I'll make this call, then you go, okay?"

"You're the boss."

She pointed him to her TV room, and he sat down on the sofa. She flipped off the television that played quietly in the background. "Want Coke, tea, water?" she asked.

"No, I'm good." He wiped his palms on the knees of his jeans.

Allie dropped her head, her guilt strong. She liked having Chase with her; it felt comfortable. He was sensitive without being soft, strong without being threatening.

She held up the phone clutched in her hand. "Guess I need to do this." She exhaled.

"Before it gets too late," Chase agreed.

She punched in the number. The phone rang on the other end. She stared at Chase. Somebody in St. Louis picked up.

"Hello."

"This is Allie Wilson calling from Harper Springs, North Carolina. To whom am I speaking?" Chase stood and moved close so he could listen.

"Who would you like to talk to?" The female voice carried a slight accent.

Allie tilted the phone so Chase could hear.

"I'm not sure. I'm trying to find someone who might know a man named Jack Wilson. I'm his daughter."

"My name is Rose Linh."

"Do you know Jack Wilson?"

"I'm not sure I should answer to a stranger."

"But I'm not a stranger. I'm Mr. Wilson's daughter, and I desperately need to talk to him!"

"Why?"

Allie glanced at Chase, her emotions boiling. "I found a picture," she stated. "I think you're in it—you and my father. Do you know him?"

Again hesitation from the other side. "Hold on a moment."

Allie heard Rose Linh drop the phone, then the sound of another voice, but she couldn't make out the words. A few seconds later, the woman picked up the phone again.

"You bring the picture and come to St. Louis. We'll talk when you arrive."

"I can't do that!"

"You say you need to see your father, that you have a picture. How do I know that's true? You come, prove to me who you are. Maybe then I'll have some information for you."

"But I'm getting married on Saturday!"

"Come when you can."

"Is my father all right?"

"You come to St. Louis. I suggest as soon as possible; that's all I can say."

Allie searched Chase's face for help.

"Go!" he whispered. "You have no choice!"

Allie focused again on the phone. "Would you give me an address, please?"

Chase grabbed a pen from a table by the sofa and wrote the address on his palm as Allie repeated it from Rose Linh.

"I'll call tomorrow after I can make flight arrangements," Allie told her.

"Good."

Allie punched off the phone and collapsed on the sofa, her body weary, her emotions wrung out. Chase perched beside her on the sofa arm.

"I don't know what to do," Allie moaned. "Trey will go ballistic if I go to St. Louis, probably Mom too. But how can I drop this now?"

"You can wait until after the honeymoon."

Allie considered the possibility but sensed that she didn't have that much time. Whatever her dad wanted her to know, she had to learn before the wedding.

"I feel like I'm being squeezed between a tank and a dump truck," she said. "Something bad will happen no matter which way I go."

She faced Chase, grateful for his presence. "What would you do?" she asked.

"You know what I want you to do," he said.

"Whatever upsets Trey, right?"

"I'm not without motive, I admit it." He smiled.

She pulled her feet under her. "No, really," she said. "What would you do?"

"It's not fair for me to answer, because I can't without bias."

"But how would a believer deal with something like this? That's what I'm asking."

Chase chewed the end of his thumb for a moment. "A believer asks for God's direction," he said.

"But how?"

"Through prayer, the advice of trusted friends, Scripture."

"But how does a believer know when the answer comes?"

Chase smiled. "You're asking tough questions. Sometimes you don't know until you look back and see how it's all worked out."

"So you don't get a blinding revelation—messages written in the clouds?"

"Some people say they do; not me though. I just ask, then listen real hard, then act on what I believe I hear."

"But what if you've got a million voices speaking to you?"

"Then you need to go see Trey the psychologist."

Allie laughed, and it felt good.

"Listen," Chase said, shifting a little closer to her. "I believe that if we'll put ourselves in a quiet place and seek God's heart and then keep our ears wide open, a lot of the voices will gradually fade away. We'll end up with only a couple of voices talking—one beckoning this way, the other that way. Then, at least in my case, I can usually find a false note in one of the voices, something that doesn't quite ring true. Once I hear that false note, I know what to do."

"And that always works?"

He shrugged. "Who knows about always? I've just got thirty-five years on record."

Allie rubbed her eyes. "I've got some thinking to do," she said.

"I expect so. Should I leave now?"

"Let's have some coffee first. I don't want you falling asleep headed back home."

After Chase left, Allie stepped onto her deck, a fresh cup of coffee in hand, and stared in the direction of the interstate where Chase was heading. Although she knew she shouldn't, she wished he were still with her. She gazed at the twinkling stars. Quiet fell. She placed her coffee on the railing and leaned on her elbows. Several minutes passed. A soft breeze feathered her face and hair. The smell of honeysuckle blanketed the air. She concentrated on shutting out every sound except the whisper of her heart. Gradually the inner distractions became fewer. The opinions of her mom, her friends, even Chase slowly faded away. Everything calmed in her soul. Allie peered deeper into the sky, something beckoning her upward, farther than she'd ever gazed. Now, as she looked past the heavens, only two impressions remained: Trey's and one she recognized only dimly, like a vague whisper from the edges of the universe—the voice of her father.

Trey said, "It's all silliness. Be logical."

Her father said, "Be open. Follow your heart."

Trey said, "You're at a transition point, a natural time for old hurts to arise. But that's all this is."

Her father said, "Life is more than logic. It's also mystery, miracle."

Trey said, "Your father is dead."

Her father said, "I'm alive."

Trey said, "If you go, I fear for us."

Her father said, "If you don't go, I fear for you."

Trey said, "Do what I say."

Her father said, "Do what you believe will bring you peace."

Allie heard the false note, and it broke her heart. She wiped her eyes as the tears formed but knew instantly what she needed to do. Tomorrow morning, as early as possible, she would make one more phone call. What happened after that only the stars, God, whoever, could know.

10

Allie found Gladys in bed when she dropped by Monday morning. Dark circles surrounded Gladys's eyes, and her skin was pale. Her hands trembled as Allie sat down beside her.

"What's wrong, Mom?" she asked.

"Just feeling weak. You know how I can get."

Allie kissed her on the forehead. "I'll get you some breakfast," she offered.

"No, I'm fine really." Gladys pushed up as if to get out of bed, but Allie gently forced her back down.

"You stay right here," she insisted.

Gladys closed her eyes, and Allie hurried to the kitchen, quickly prepared toast with jam, tea, and a bowl of fruit, and hauled it back to Gladys on a tray.

"I know you don't eat when you get like this," she said, setting the food on the bed.

She handed Gladys a piece of toast. "You've had too much on you lately," Allie continued as Gladys nibbled.

"Maybe so."

"I know so."

Allie opened a window and turned on the overhead fan

as Gladys ate another few bites. "Need some air in here," Allie said.

Gladys sipped from the tea, then put the cup on the tray. "What are you doing out so early?" she asked, patting the bed for Allie to sit.

Allie eased close to Gladys. Although she feared her timing, she couldn't lie about what had happened. "I'm going to St. Louis today," she said, anxious and excited at the same time.

Gladys's eyes widened, and Allie continued. "I may have found Dad."

Gladys sat up straighter, fluffing her pillow behind her back. Allie quickly filled her in on all that had transpired in the past few days. How she had visited Walt Mason, read the letter from her dad, visited the safety deposit box in Asheville, found the picture with the phone number, and talked to the Vietnamese woman in St. Louis. She kept her eyes fixed on her mom as she talked, hopeful she wouldn't push her over the edge with so much news. When she finished, Gladys folded her arms over her chest and clenched her jaw.

"You did all this without telling me a thing!" she accused.

"I worried about you . . . didn't think I should say anything until I knew more."

"I always hoped you wouldn't do this," Gladys said, "but I guess it was inevitable."

"Probably so."

"What does Trey say?"

"He's not happy; I haven't told him about my plan to go to St. Louis."

Gladys shook her head. "This won't be good."

"What else can I do?"

"You know the answer to that."

"No, I don't."

"You could lose Trey if you insist on this."

"Not if he really loves me."

Gladys studied Allie for several seconds. "You're willing to take that chance, aren't you?" Surprise rode her voice.

"I suppose I am."

Gladys stared toward the window. "Did you bring the picture with you?" she asked.

Allie produced it from her purse and handed it over, and Gladys inspected it and then gave it back to Allie. "Jack never said what happened in Vietnam," she whispered. "I imagined all sorts of things but never this."

"You think it's true, then? Dad took a Vietnamese wife?"

"Look at that girl's eyes, dark as yours, your dad's."

"But you said he loved us!" Allie stood.

"He did! I know that!"

"Then there's got to be another explanation, something we can't see or understand."

"I can't imagine what that is."

Allie sat back down. "I have to find out," she said. "And I have to do it now."

"The letter suggests he's already dead."

"Yes."

"But you think he's alive."

Allie nodded.

"But why? Nothing indicates that."

Allie wanted to tell Gladys about the voices from the deck, how the one in her heart told her to keep going, that her dad was alive. But she didn't know how to explain it, so she said, "I just know it, that's all."

"You're making a mistake."

"I'm willing to take the risk."

"I hope it's worth it."

Allie lay down by her mom and hugged her close. "We both need to know," she said. "One way or the other."

Gladys closed her eyes. "I'm tired," she said.

"I'll be back as soon as I can," Allie said.

"Will you talk to Trey before you go?"

"Of course."

"I hope he understands."

"Me too."

Allie said the words, but they sounded hollow the instant they fell from her tongue.

Eight hours later Allie stuffed a bag into the overhead luggage bin on a plane to St. Louis, plopped wearily into the window seat, and snapped her seatbelt for takeoff. Chase sat beside her, his feet edged toward the aisle.

Allie shook her head at Chase. "You really shouldn't be here," she said.

"I know."

Allie's shoulders slumped with grief as she recalled her visit with Trey that morning. He was already at their house in his painting clothes when she'd reached him. He'd held a paintbrush as she told him of the phone call to St. Louis and advised him of her plans to take a quick trip to see if her dad was alive. Trey had slammed the paintbrush into the can as she finished.

"This is unbelievable!" he'd stammered. "You're going halfway across the country just five days before the wedding to find a father you haven't seen since before you started school?"

"But everything for the wedding is in order!" she'd argued. "All you and I have to do is show up on Friday and Saturday!"

"This house isn't finished!" he'd reminded her, waving toward the ceiling.

"We've got our whole lives to finish the house!"

He'd spun on his heel, then faced her again. "You going with this Chase guy?"

"I want you to go with me," she'd tried to soothe him. "Just a day, then right back. I want you there."

He'd picked his paintbrush back up and shook his head. "Can't do it."

"But my dad might still be alive."

"Not from the sound of the letter he wrote."

"But I can't be sure."

He'd held the brush at his side. "This is your quest, not mine."

She'd moved to him, taken the brush from his hand, and wrapped an arm around his waist. He'd stayed still, sphinx-like. "It should be our quest," she'd said. "Don't you see? This is important to me, so it should be important to you too."

"Finishing this house is important to me, should be important to you too."

"But the two things don't compare!" She'd backed away and clenched her fists at her sides.

"To me they do. My folks lived in this house, my grandparents before them. My mom gave it to us for our wedding; all we have to do is renovate it. To leave it now, before we finish it, seems wrong, disrespectful. We said we'd do this together, but you haven't . . . haven't kept your part in that bargain. It makes me wonder if you're always going to be undependable."

Allie had felt shocked. "I don't get it," she'd said.

"What's to get?"

"You're a psychologist, you help people, you're sensitive to people. But . . . here . . . now . . ." Allie had grasped for words. "You're comparing a house, even one as sentimental as this one, to a person's father, *my* father? How can somebody trained in human emotions do something like that? It seems so . . . so cold, so . . . uncaring."

Trey had closed his eyes, then opened them again and gazed at her. "You're distancing yourself from me," he'd said softly. "I don't know why, and I can't do anything to stop you, but all of this—the whole matter of your dad—it feels too unreal, too random for it to be anything but that."

"But I'm not. I—"

He'd held up the paintbrush to stop her. "Think about it on your trip," he'd suggested. "See if there's not some truth in what I'm saying."

Allie had almost reached for him again, but he'd waved the paintbrush, indicating she should go.

"I'll be back by the end of the day," she'd offered.

"I'll be here."

"We'll talk then."

"That will be good."

"Trey?"

He'd squatted down to the paint can, then looked up and smiled. She'd rushed to him, kissed him on the forehead, then hurried from the house before she'd started to cry.

Now, on the plane with Chase, Allie still couldn't make

sense of what had happened between her and Trey in the past two weeks. Right now it seemed that Chase understood her while Trey didn't, that Chase seemed to care about her feelings more than Trey did, that Chase seemed—and she really hated to admit this—steadier, more grounded, more substantial than Trey. Add a sense of humor to that, not to mention his good looks, and . . . She pushed away the thought.

"I can't believe I'm doing this," she said to Chase.

"It's not what I saw in my future a week ago either."

The plane lifted off.

"I'm getting married Saturday," she said.

"So I've heard."

She shook her head.

"What?" Chase asked.

"Trey suggested I was using this search for my dad to distance myself from him."

"Are you?"

She stared out the window as the clouds rose beside her. "No."

"Then he's wrong. You'll see him tomorrow, make up with him, walk down the aisle on Saturday, and live happily ever after."

"What will that do to your idea that I'm supposed to marry you?"

"Blow a hole the size of this jet in it."

Allie stared out the window for a few seconds, then said, "What if I'm not the one using this to create distance between us?" she asked.

"You're suggesting Trey is doing what he's blaming you of doing?"

"You think that's possible?"

"They're cloning babies now; anything is possible."

"But he's a therapist; he should know it if that's what he's doing."

"A doctor always makes the worst patient."

Allie folded her hands and played with the possibility. Could Trey be looking for a way out of the marriage, even at this late date? Was he using this conflict to express his discontent with her? To create distance between them without feeling any blame? But didn't he love her? Yes, she had faults. She procrastinated too much, she got moody every now and again, a stubborn streak ran up her backbone, and she could show a temper occasionally. But was that enough to make Trey break up with her?

"It's scary," she said.

"What's the worst that can happen?"

"Trey can call off the wedding, that's what!"

Chase shrugged. "That's not the end of the world."

"Not to you, maybe."

"So it's embarrassing. You return some wedding presents, and you're out some cash. But think of the other side of it."

"What side?"

"If you marry Trey and then find out down the road that you weren't right for each other. What's that going to cost you—in terms of hurt, embarrassment, dollars even?"

Allie rubbed her forehead. "Do you believe in a one and only when it comes to love? A soul mate, as people say it today?"

Chase brushed back his hair. "I believe in a perfect will of God; if we find that, we'll find the person we're supposed to spend our lives with."

"But what if we mess it up? Humans do that, you know.

What if we don't find that perfect will of God? Are we doomed to misery the rest of our lives?"

"Don't think so. If we look to God for guidance, God will help us take what we've chosen and find joy in it. Perhaps not the ultimate joy we could have had, but joy just the same."

Allie's brow furrowed, and Chase continued. "Let me give you an example. Imagine life is a trip." He leaned closer as he talked. "Sometimes you drive along on the main highway. That's the best highway—widest lanes, best views, brightest lights, highest quality restaurants, easiest traffic, straightest route to your destination. So long as you stay on that highway, everything is great. But suppose you make a wrong turn somewhere—maybe you got confused, maybe you got misdirected, but you head off on another route. This road has potholes all over it, wrecks here and there, bandits along the way, briars and brambles growing up along the sides. You're still headed toward your destination, but this road twists and turns and goes through all kinds of trouble to get there."

"So God's perfect will is the main highway?"

"You're so smart."

"And the other way is what happens when we step out of God's perfect will."

"Exactly."

"We're not doomed on it; we can still find our way in life, but without quite as much ease, joy, and satisfaction as we would have experienced if we'd stayed on the main highway."

"You got it."

"God doesn't desert us on the other road?"

"Of course not."

Allie leaned back. "It makes some sense," she said.

"Glad to be of help."

Her headache softened a little.

"One other thought," Chase said.

"Are we taking another highway?"

He grinned. "Not exactly. Have you considered that maybe God is using this search for your dad to create the space between you and Trey?"

"So you can squeeze through it?"

"Forget about me. Think about you and Trey."

Allie mulled the matter over. "You're saying God brought this situation to me so Trey and I could go through this conflict to discover we're not meant for each other?"

"I'm just raising the question—I don't have a clue what the answer is."

"But that's saying that finding my dad is a means to an end."

"That's possible. Or one more thing . . ."

"My head is spinning."

"Last thought, I promise."

"Okay."

"Suppose it's both. God wants you to find out about your dad. That stands on its own. But while you're going through that, you also find out about you and Trey. God didn't create the one for the other, but God uses the one, as it happens, to reveal the other."

The flight attendant approached and offered them a drink, and Allie and Chase asked for water. The attendant handed over the water and some peanuts and walked off. Allie opened the water bottle, swallowed a big drink, and faced Chase again.

"What about you?" she asked, eager to escape the spotlight for a second.

"What about me?"

"Your love life, God's perfect will."

He ripped open his peanuts. "Not much to say."

"But you had somebody special in your life. What happened to her?"

"I'm eating my peanuts," he said, holding up the bag. "Can't talk with my mouth full."

"You know all kinds of stuff about me and Trey," she protested. "Time for you to spill some beans."

He washed his peanuts down with the rest of his water and dropped his eyes. "It's nothing too dramatic," he said.

"Bore me, then. We've got two hours."

"One or the other of us missed God's will," he said. "To this day, I still don't know which."

"Explain, please."

"She lived in Nashville, a lawyer. Cheryl Booth. I knew her from college. We dated for two years; I thought we were ready for the next level. I bought a ring. But when I got down on my knees, she pulled me back up and said that was as good a time as any to inform me she didn't think it would work."

"Why not?"

He licked his lips. "Seems my lifestyle wasn't what she wanted."

"Your lifestyle?"

"A carpenter—too low on the social ladder for her liking."

"She said that to you?"

"Not in so many words, but I knew that's what she meant when she said our lifestyles didn't match."

"But don't you make a decent living?"

"Yes, you'd be surprised. And I told her I'd move to

Nashville, rent a shop, do designer furniture. That wasn't enough. I didn't understand it then, but looking back, I can see her point. She needed somebody comfortable in a tuxedo, somebody smooth with politicians, lobbyists, high and mighty folks. I never would have enjoyed that."

"So she did you a favor?"

"If tearing a man's heart out is a favor, yes, she's a heck of a gal."

Allie smiled lightly. "Did she prevent you from finding God's will, or did she set you loose to find it?"

"She set me loose to wait for you, so I guess it's the latter."

"But I'm going to marry Trey."

"Then why am I here and not him?"

Allie's headache returned, and she leaned against the seat. "I still haven't exactly figured that one out."

Chase laughed, and Allie relaxed for a moment. "I'm glad you came," she said.

"Another chance for me to weasel my way into your heart," he said.

"No, seriously, you didn't have to do this. When I called you, after Trey said no, I realize you had to rearrange some things."

"I didn't want you alone in this," he said. "I did what any friend would do, especially one who wants to marry you."

"One thing at a time," she said softly. "Let's find my dad then worry about that."

"A good idea."

Allie drank the rest of her water and closed her eyes. In a couple of hours, she would talk to Rose Linh. If that went well, she might know where to find her father by the time the sun broke on a new day. That was worry enough for one trip.

11

The plane landed at just past six, and Allie and Chase climbed off, got their rental car, and headed straight for Rose Linh's house, Chase behind the wheel.

"I told her we could get there about seven thirty," Allie explained as she pored over the hand-drawn map she'd sketched with the directions.

"You navigate, and I'll pilot."

They fell into quiet as they made their way in and out of St. Louis traffic, both of them lost in their own ruminations. A light rain fell outside, and Chase switched on the wipers. Allie glanced at him and smiled shyly. No matter what else came from this, she'd found a genuine friend.

Thirty minutes later they reached the street where Rose Linh lived, and Chase pulled the car to a stop in front of the number the woman had given Allie. Small, square houses, a couple of bedrooms at most, squeezed in together on the street. A few trees grew in some of the yards but not many, and no sidewalks led from the street to the houses. The yards were largely weeds. There were tufts of grass growing here and there but not much. A gaggle of young men wearing skull caps stood by a rundown car in a yard two houses down, apparently oblivious to the misty rain.

Most of them held cigarettes, the smoke from their lips rising into the air. They stared at Chase and Allie, their gaze a cross between bored and belligerent.

"I'm glad you came with me," Allie told Chase.

"I know." He patted her hand, and his touch warmed her, but she gritted her teeth against it.

"It's time," she said.

"You ready?"

She climbed out and hustled through the square yard to the front door, Chase right behind.

A petite woman about her age opened the door before they made it to the front steps. She wore a blue-jean skirt, a pullover pink sweater, and simple black pumps. Her haircut surrounded her round face.

"My name is Rose Linh," she said.

Allie introduced herself, then Chase.

"Please come in," Rose Linh said, pointing them through the door.

Allie and Chase walked through, Rose Linh following. She directed them to a small but neatly tended sitting area to the right. Allie perched on the edge of a sofa, Chase beside her. Rose Linh took a spot in a wicker chair across from Allie. The room smelled fresh, like lemon. Allie folded her hands and inspected Rose Linh toe to head. Tiny feet, slender frame, hands like a doll's, smooth skin, round face, eyes Asian but cheeks and mouth more American—definitely the offspring of an American and a Vietnamese. Just as obviously, she'd assimilated into American ways, the language, the clothing, even her name, Rose. Allie looked into her eyes and again felt the odd sensation of having seen them before. A touch of resentment hit her again—how could her dad do such a thing?

Rose Linh spoke. "You say you're Jack Wilson's daughter."

"Yes."

"You bring the picture?"

Allie pulled several pictures from her purse and handed them to Rose Linh, who smiled slightly as she examined them and then handed them back to Allie.

"You're definitely his daughter," Rose Linh said. "Same tall body, long fingers, black eyes."

"You also have black eyes," Allie said, almost breathless.

Rose Linh tilted her head slightly, and her eyes brightened. "You think I'm also Jack Wilson's daughter?"

Allie shrugged and tried to look indifferent, but her stomach churned inside. Rose Linh suddenly stood and walked from the room, and Allie wondered if she'd insulted her in some manner she didn't understand. She looked at Chase, but he had nothing to offer. A clock ticked somewhere in the background. Allie tried to stay calm by inspecting the room. Thin lamps sat on two tables. A painting of a thatched jungle hut hung over the wicker chair. Rose Linh reentered, an older woman before her. The woman walked with a limp, but Allie figured her not much older than her own mother.

Chase stood as the older woman entered, but Rose Linh waved him back down. "This is Nu Than, my mother," she said. "She will make it all clear to you."

Nu Than brushed back her hair, and Allie noticed gray at the temples. Wrinkles curled around her eyes, and her hands shook a little as she placed them in her lap. She glanced at Rose Linh, then focused on Allie.

"You have face of Jack Wilson," Nu Than said, her English

choppy, with a much stronger accent than Rose Linh's. "The eyes most of all."

Allie wanted to scream at her to say what she most needed to hear. Had her father sired Rose Linh?

"Rose Linh is not sister to you," Nu Than said.

Allie exhaled, but her heart still pounded.

"Rose Linh is daughter of an American man your father killed in black of night many years ago."

Allie recoiled, and Chase put a hand over hers.

Nu Than waited as if to give Allie a moment to recover, but she couldn't find her voice, so Nu Than continued. "Jack Wilson, he feel terrible about the killing, thought he responsible for us, so he give us money before he leave. We had to wait two years, but then . . . we use the money to come here."

Chase squeezed Allie's hands as she tried to make sense of what she'd just heard. An American had fathered Rose Linh, so how had her father killed him? Nu Than kept talking.

"A year ago, Jack Wilson found us. Said a cousin of mine, Vietnamese man, see him when he visit Dinh Tuong. Told him where to find us. He come by with some money to give to us. Still carry guilt over the years that pass."

Nu Than paused, and Allie tried to get a handle on her emotions. "He left us," Allie whispered. "My mother said he didn't feel worthy of us. He drank . . . fell into black moods, depression."

"Because he killed my father," Rose Linh said.

"But how?"

Nu Than peered at her hands in her lap and began to speak, her tone soft, almost reverent. "Billy Trotter, I fell in love with him. It happened some in those days. GI boys lonely; Vietnam girls eager to please the Americans. Billy Trotter took up with me, spent many nights at my house." She wiped a tear away, then continued. "Billy Trotter at my house that night, the Vietcong raid a couple of hours before light. Billy Trotter rise from sleep, grab his rifle, run into the dark barefoot, still wearing the black pajamas I gave him for his sleeping."

Allie tried to imagine the scene.

"Night black, much confusion, smoke from many weapons, mortar fire, men running all over, women screaming, babies crying, machine guns blasting."

Allie sensed the climax of the story.

"Jack Wilson, your father, and other GIs, they pour into the village, coming for the Vietcong. Billy Trotter run out of village toward them. Jack Wilson, your father, he shoot at whatever moves. Billy Trotter in black pajamas, smoke everywhere, Jack Wilson, your father, he and his men fire into the village, and Billy Trotter falls dead outside my hut."

Nu Than stared into Allie's eyes. "The Vietcong run away; daylight comes. I find Jack Wilson and Walt Mason by Billy Trotter, his head in your father's lap, his eyes already empty, your father's eyes too—empty as broken bottles."

Allie bowed her head. It all made sense now.

"The rest of the time your father stay in Vietnam, he come to care for me and Rose Linh every time possible. He bring us things, give us money—do what he can to make it better for us."

"The Marines pressed no charges against him?" Allie asked softly.

Nu Than shook her head. "He tell me he was cleared of any blame. Billy Trotter not where he should have been.

Marines blame Billy Trotter instead of your father. I know that is right, your father not to blame. Bad things happen in war, things no man can avoid or fix when they come."

"But my father felt guilty the rest of his life anyway."

"Jack Wilson a man with a big heart."

Allie looked at Chase, then back to Nu Than. "You say he gave you money?"

"Yes, before he left, he visited one last time, brought all the money he had. Told us he thought Vietcong sure to win. His money paid for us to come here."

Allie focused on Rose Linh. "So you grew up in America."

"Since I was a little girl."

Allie tried to soak everything in.

"Jack Wilson tell me of his last trip to Vietnam," Nu Than said.

Allie's eyes widened. "He did?"

"He went back to my old village, to the place where Billy Trotter fell dead."

"Tell me what happened."

Nu Than smiled gently. "Your father tell me that he and Walt Mason hire a jeep, drive into the north country, through the mountains. The place not much changed, he say. He climb out of the jeep, walk into the jungle, overgrown now, the signs of war almost gone. But he say he was still able to find the spot, a small clearing on a hill. Billy Trotter fell there. Your father and Walt Mason, they go to the clearing, Walt Mason then drop back some. Your father, he walk to the spot, hang his head, and stand a long time. Your father kneels, both knees in the dirt. He take up two handfuls of the earth, pour it over his head, almost like ashes. The dirt slide through his hair, over his face. Tears mingle as it passes his eyes. Your father fall on his face in the dirt, his hands grabbing the ground. He lay there still for more time. The sun begins to drop, a light breeze blows in the air. Your father moves, kneels on one knee, and digs for a moment with his hands. Then he takes something from his pocket. He tell me it was a little cross, he never tell me where he got it. He kisses the cross three times, then lays it in the little hole he dug where his tears mixed with the earth. He covers the cross with the ground, and then he pats the dirt and stands. He wipes his eyes and walks away."

Allie sat motionless. No wonder her father had suffered so much. She felt so hurt for him, so grieved. Was this what he wanted her to know? Was this why she'd embarked on this quest?

She looked at Chase and he smiled, and she felt comforted. Yet something still remained to be discovered. She faced Nu Than again.

"Do you know where he is now?" she asked. "If he's still alive?"

Nu Than shook her head, and Allie's heart fell. "He disappear again after he visit us. Not seen him since."

"Was he okay when he left? Did he seem healthy?"

Nu Than pondered the question for several moments. "He seem happier," she finally said. "Like something good, something important, happen to him. But his health not the best, I think. He breathe heavy a lot, I see him holding his chest some, like he hurt inside. He not say anything, but I get the feeling . . . I don't know . . . that the journey to Vietnam, the visit to where Billy Trotter fell . . . that journey was to be his last. I believe he know that too."

"He went to Vietnam seeking absolution," Chase said, speaking for the first time since they entered the house.

Allie faced him, and he explained.

"Your father wanted forgiveness," Chase said, "so he returned to the spot where he believes he committed his greatest sin. It's a practice repeated in all kinds of religions."

"That what he say to me when he comes here last year," Nu Than said. "He says to me, 'Forgive me.' 'I did a long time ago,' I say to him."

"What happens after forgiveness?" Allie asked, although she already suspected the answer.

"New life," Chase said. "Or death."

"So Dad came home to die?"

"A forgiven man doesn't fear death," Chase said.

"The cross," Allie said. "The one he buried."

"Was your dad a believer?" Chase asked.

"Not that I know of," Allie said.

"Maybe he became one."

"It's possible."

Silence fell, and Allie wondered again if this was it—what her dad wanted to communicate to her. Somehow, in spite of all she'd learned, she still felt something missing, one more piece of the puzzle. If her father had died, what had killed him? He was only fifty-three, so even if he had a heart condition as the letter mentioned, that was still extremely young. Had his drinking made matters worse? That was possible, but she still didn't feel satisfied. If her dad was dead, she wanted to know it for certain. And more than that, she wanted to know if he had indeed died at peace. But what else could she do? She faced Nu Than once more.

"I thank you for what you've told me," she said.

"Your father a well-intentioned man," Nu Than said. "I

never feel no harm toward him. Billy Trotter's death was accident of war."

Allie stood, moved to Nu Than, and hugged her. Rose Linh smiled as Allie straightened and took her hand.

"Will you continue the search for your father?" Rose Linh asked.

"If I can."

"If you find him, tell him again that we thank him for his kindnesses to us."

"I'll do that."

She and Chase left then, Allie's heart glad for what she'd learned but still confused and hurt that she hadn't found her dad.

"What next?" she asked Chase as they climbed into the car to go back to the airport.

"I guess you better go home and get married."

"I suppose you're right."

He started the car and pulled it onto the street. Allie wondered what Trey was doing, thinking, wanting. Although her quest for her dad had apparently ended, her problems had by no means concluded. She propped her head against the window and wanted to cry. A heavier rain began to fall. She felt hollow, like somebody had yanked her heart out with bare hands. Something wasn't right, wasn't right with Trey, wasn't right with her dad. But what else could she do?

"Why did all this happen?" she said softly. "What was the purpose in it?"

"Some people believe that everything happens for a reason," Chase said.

"So what's the reason for the past two weeks? If it wasn't to find my dad, then what?"

"You'll have to answer that," Chase said.

Allie tried to figure it out. Was it so she could meet Chase? But why? So she could discover something about Trey? But what—except that they had some things they had to straighten out before their wedding? What a mess!

Chase's cell phone rang, and he picked it up from the console. "Yeah," he said.

Allie stared out the window and tried to ignore the conversation.

"Wow!" he said.

Unable to stop herself, she faced him. His mouth hung open. She heard his dad's voice on the other end but couldn't make out what he said.

"Really?" Chase glanced at Allie; his face gave nothing away, but Allie's heart roared anyway. Something told her that life had just changed—for better or worse, she didn't know.

"You think we should come home or go straight there?" Chase asked.

Allie tried to hear but couldn't make out anything.

"Okay," Chase said. "We'll go immediately."

He hung up and faced Allie. "You won't believe it," he said.

"What?" she demanded.

"Your father."

"Yes?"

"He's alive."

Allie stopped breathing. "You're sure?"

"My dad says so. You know he's been checking around through the VA. Seems that a buddy of his, a doctor at a

VA hospital in Atlanta, called an hour ago, said your dad was there."

Allie's mind bounced in all directions. She wanted to scream and shout and cry all at the same time. She closed her eyes and sought to steady herself. Chase pulled the car into a gas station lot and parked. Allie began to sob.

"Hey," Chase soothed, touching her forearm. "This is good, right? No time for crying."

"I just can't believe it."

Chase found a tissue and gently dabbed at her wet face. "It's a crazy world," he said.

Allie smiled at him, and her spirits lifted. "Should I go home first? Talk to Mom?"

"Dad seemed to think we best go to Atlanta pretty fast."

"So it's critical?"

"Sounded serious, yes."

Allie considered her mom, then Trey. "Trey's going to kill me," she said.

"Not if he really loves you."

"I need to call Mom," she said, "ask her to meet me there."

"That sounds reasonable."

Allie wiped her eyes. "So we're going to Atlanta?"

"As soon as a jet can fly us there."

She smiled again. "I knew I'd find him," she said.

"Almost makes you believe in miracles, huh?"

"I wouldn't go that far yet."

"But maybe someday?"

Allie tried to imagine the possibility. Did miracles really happen? Had God brought her to this moment? Or was

167

it something much more coincidental—mindless chance, sheer undirected fate? It was the same question she'd asked since this started, but she still had no answer.

"Drive," she said. "We'll worry about miracles later."

Chase chuckled and obeyed, and Allie's heart soared higher than the jet they would soon take to see her father.

12

They caught the last plane of the day from St. Louis to Atlanta and landed at just past 1:00 a.m. It took almost an hour after they landed in Atlanta for them to rent a car and drive to the VA hospital. By the time they arrived, Allie's emotions had taken enough back-and-forth trips to earn frequent flyer miles. Fear, joy, anxiety, hope, love, anger, fear again—all rolled through her heart over and over again.

Her phone call to Trey—made while she waited in St. Louis for the flight to Atlanta—hadn't gone well. Although he'd said he was glad she'd found her dad, he'd also said he couldn't join her in Atlanta to see him. Too many things going on, he'd told her, too much confusion for both of them to be out of town. She'd assured him she agreed with his decision but inwardly had felt hurt by it. What kind of man refused to join his fiancée the day she found her long-lost father? Was that the kind of man she wanted to marry?

Unable to convince Trey to join her, she'd called Gladys. To her surprise, her mom had taken the news more calmly than she'd expected. "I'll come as quickly as I can in the morning," Gladys had said.

"You want me to wait on you to see him?" Allie had asked.

"No, you go to him the second you arrive."

Allie had agreed and hung up.

Now she climbed out of the rental car and made her way into the entrance of the VA hospital about seven miles east of downtown Atlanta. An attendant at the information desk gave her a room number and pointed her and Chase to the elevators. Stepping in, she faced Chase and held out her hands for him to see.

"You're shaking," he said, pointing to her fingers.

"I know." She shoved her hands into her pants pockets. "Do you blame me?"

He put a hand on her shoulder. "It will all be fine," he said. "This is what you wanted, right, what you set out to do—find your dad before your wedding?"

"I couldn't have done it without you," she said.

"Sure you could, but I'm glad I was here anyway."

The elevator dinged and stopped. Time seemed to halt as they waited for the door to open. Allie took Chase's hand and held it in both of hers.

"You still think I'm the woman you're supposed to marry?" she asked.

He raised his right eyebrow. "Strange time to ask that," he said.

"Strange time for a lot of things."

"Yeah."

She felt a sudden urge to be held and wanted Chase to pull her close and hug her tightly, but the elevator door opened before that could happen, and she dropped his hand and stepped out, her heart riddled with a mixture of guilt and excitement. Right now, however, she had no time to figure out what those emotions meant or where they might lead.

Chase halted as the elevator door closed. "You need to go without me from here," he said.

Allie nodded, and Chase pointed to a sign that said "Waiting Room" a few steps away. "I'll be right there," he said.

Allie bit her lip. "Thanks," she said. "For everything."

"Go to your dad," he ordered.

She smiled, then hurried down the hallway to room 312.

Allie entered the room softly, the door making only a light swishing sound as she pushed it open and then shut it behind her. Her dad slept in his bed, tubes and wires attached to him in a number of spots. She waited for her eyes to adjust to the dim lighting and for her heart to slow to a manageable pace. Her dad's breath came in shallow gasps, and he stirred every few seconds. For what seemed like the millionth time in the last two weeks, Allie pondered the meaning of her search but once more reached no definite conclusion about its purpose. What good was it to see her dad if he was going to die within days, if not sooner?

Her dad moaned lightly, and she stepped closer and just stood there for several minutes, the only sounds those of his breathing and the monitors clicking around his body. Finally, when she didn't think she could take it any longer, his eyes suddenly blinked and opened. Allie almost ran away, but something held her glued to the spot. Another minute passed while they just stared at each other. Allie wondered if her dad was conscious, if he comprehended anything. But then he spoke.

"Who are you?" His voice rasped as if dragging the words over sharp rocks.

Allie rubbed her eyes but couldn't find her voice.

Her dad lifted a hand and motioned her closer. She obeyed, unable to do anything else. She stopped as his arm relaxed on his bed, the movement seeming to tire him. She studied his eyes, still fixed on her. Black eyes, like hockey pucks indeed. Black olives, onyx stones, coal—name the blackest object ever created, and the color of his eyes matched it.

His eyes widened slightly and seemed to light up at least ten watts. "You're Allie," he whispered.

"Yes," she said, finding her voice.

"Is Gladys with you?"

"On her way."

A smile briefly crossed his face. "How did you . . . find me?"

"It's a long story, but I've been searching for you."

"Why?"

She wanted to tell him the full tale but didn't know if she had the time. "Let's just say I felt driven to it," she said.

He didn't press her further. "I'm not sure . . . sure I want you here," he said.

"Why not?"

"I . . . don't deserve it."

Her heart went out to him, and she grabbed a chair and sat down by the bed. They now gazed at each other from the same level. "Sure you do," she said. "I know why you stayed away from us. I found Nu Than and Rose Linh. They told me everything. You've suffered enough for Billy Trotter's death; it was an accident, the fog of war."

He slowly shook his head. "I let it eat me up," he said. "Let it become an excuse . . . drank . . . my fault for that. Guilt over . . . Vietnam, then guilt over . . . drinking, deserting you and your mom. It got worse . . . and I didn't stop it." He closed his eyes, obviously weary from talking.

"But you couldn't help it," she said. "Alcoholism is a disease."

"That's too easy!" he rasped, his voice stronger for an instant. "Drinking is a choice that becomes a disease, not the other way around! I wronged you, your mom, everyone who knew me."

Allie wanted to argue more but figured it wasn't the time. One of the monitors attached to her dad clicked. He spoke again. "I'm glad . . . you came," he said. "Whether I deserve it or not."

"You're not alone," she assured him. "I'm here; Mom will be soon."

He coughed. When he spoke again, his voice sounded a touch better, like he'd gathered energy from some resource deep inside. "I need your forgiveness."

"You have it," she said.

He shook his head. "It's not that easy," he said. "You've got anger, resentment at me; I don't blame you. Forgiveness will take a long time, maybe years, but I need to hear that you want to do it, want to try."

Allie's eyes watered. "I do," she assured him.

He closed his eyes again. His breath slowed, became shallower, then seemed to stop for an instant. Allie squeezed his hand but got little response.

"Dad?"

No response.

"Dad?"

His eyes popped open.

"Two more things," he whispered.

"What?"

He held up a finger as if making a necessary point. "The Lord . . . that's settled for me."

"You're a believer?"

"A sorry one, but . . . yes; that's how I stopped . . . drinking."

Allie wanted to ask what led him to faith but saw he didn't have the strength.

"Another thing," he whispered. "What's killing me, you need to know it."

"What is it, Dad?"

"Don't know . . . details. Talk to the doctor. But you may . . . have it."

"What?"

"It's genetic, handed down. Some fancy name."

"I don't understand."

His eyes bored into hers. "Talk to the doctor, he'll tell you . . . get tested . . . it's treatable if you find it early enough."

"Okay."

"Final thing."

"What?"

He reached for her face, touched her forehead, ran his fingers down her nose, held her chin. "Your eyes . . . you've got your daddy's eyes."

He sagged back then, obviously spent. Allie wanted to ask him more but didn't dare. As weak as he was, he might die before her mom arrived if she pressed him harder. The door suddenly swished open, and a nurse entered the room.

"I'm Ginny," said the nurse, a thin black woman with a bright smile and straight teeth.

Allie quickly introduced herself.

Ginny motioned her outside the room. Allie kissed her dad on the forehead and followed her out. Ginny closed the door behind them. Allie started to ask about her dad's disease, but Ginny spoke before she could.

"I'm glad somebody came to be with Jack," Ginny said. "We asked him over and over if he wanted us to call any family, but he always said no."

"It's been a while since I saw him," Allie said.

"I figured that."

"He left home a long time ago."

"We get a lot of Vietnam vets who suffered this way, took up drinking, drugs, after the war."

"Thanks for taking care of him."

Ginny smiled. "I saw your picture," she said.

"What?"

"In his wallet; he keeps a picture of you and a woman I figure to be your mama."

Allie's eyes brimmed.

"I prayed you here," Ginny said.

"You prayed me here?" The words sounded strange, like voodoo or something.

"Yes. I'm a believing woman, and I asked the Lord that if you and the woman in that picture were his kin, you would come see him before it was too late."

"But Dad didn't want us here."

"A patient doesn't always know what's best, you know what I mean?"

"But you do?"

"The Lord does. If the Lord wanted you here, you would come. If not . . . so be it."

"You really believe that?"

"Don't you?" She looked at Allie as if asking a baby girl

175

if she liked pink ribbons. The answer just had to be yes, but Allie wasn't ready to concede that.

"I'm not sure what to believe."

"How else you explain your being here?"

Allie tried to wrap her mind around the notion that her presence was the result of Ginny's prayers. If so . . .

She pushed away the thought but reserved the right to bring it up again at a more opportune time.

"My dad said he had some genetic disease," she said, changing the subject. "Told me I should get tested for it."

"You best see the doctor about that," Ginny said. "But maybe that's reason enough for your coming."

"How so?"

Ginny shrugged. "Maybe the Lord brought you here so Jack wouldn't die alone or maybe so you could find out about this disease you might have."

"Maybe both."

"That's a strong possibility. The Lord works in mysterious ways his wonders to perform."

Allie rubbed her eyes—she had so much to consider.

"Go on now," Ginny said. "Let me do a couple things with your dad. You come back in half an hour."

"He's okay for that long?"

Ginny nodded, and Allie thanked her again, then turned and hurried to the waiting room to find Chase and wait for her mom.

13

Jack Wilson died two days later, at just past six in the evening, with Allie on one side of his intensive-care-unit bed, Gladys on the other. Trey, who had arrived just after dinner, sat in the waiting room down the hall. Allie and her mom stayed by Jack for close to five minutes after he breathed his last, neither of them speaking. They cried quietly as tears coursed down their faces. Finally Gladys eased to Allie and put an arm around her.

"I'm glad you found him," Gladys whispered. "Glad he didn't die alone."

"Me too," Allie said, dabbing her eyes clear. "So grateful we got the chance to tell him we loved him."

"For him to tell us too."

Allie stepped to her dad one final time and kissed him on the cheek. "Rest in peace, Dad."

Gladys started crying again but also kissed Jack a last time. Then they walked out together.

"I'll go find Ginny," Gladys said.

"I best go see Trey."

"I expect you should."

Allie slouched toward the waiting room, her heart low. Trey stood as she entered the otherwise empty room, and she tried to brighten her face but didn't manage it too well.

"He's passed," she said.

Trey crossed to her and slipped an arm around her waist. "I'm sorry," he said.

Allie laid her head on his shoulder, and he held her for a long minute, then stepped back. "What do we do now?" he asked.

"I don't know, never done this before."

"I'm sure the hospital will take care of things."

"We'll bury him in Harper Springs," Allie said. "Mom and I talked about it when she got here yesterday."

Trey studied his shoes, and Allie felt the distance between them. Even though he'd finally come to Atlanta, his earlier refusal had kicked a dent in her trust in him. Until now she'd been too concerned for her dad to give their situation much thought, but now that she did, it saddened her.

"When do you think the funeral will be?" he asked.

Allie closed her eyes, the lack of sleep in the past two days catching up with her. "Friday or Saturday," she said.

"What about the wedding?" he asked.

Allie sagged onto a sofa sitting in the corner, the enormity of the moment too much to bear standing up. "I don't know," she admitted. "I don't know."

She covered her eyes with her hands and tried to figure things out. Should she marry Trey? But he'd refused to rush to her when she found her dad. How could she love him after that?

A million thoughts tumbled through her head. Could they postpone the funeral until after the wedding? But what about the honeymoon? The airline tickets, the reservations at the resort—all was ready and paid for. Could they postpone the wedding? But they had people coming in from four different states.

Allie looked back to Trey, who stood beside her, his eyes still down. Was he the man she should marry? Was he God's perfect will for her? He had his faults, sure, but what man didn't?

She thought of Chase, staying at a hotel a couple of blocks away. Although he'd stayed in Atlanta to "help wherever I can," as he put it, he'd left an hour before Trey had arrived.

"I don't want to come between you two," he'd told Allie as he left the hospital. "You decide your future with him; I'll live with your choice."

"You still think you're going to marry me?" she'd asked.

"It's in God's hands," he'd said.

She'd thanked him for all he'd done, and he'd left, his broad back the last thing she saw as he walked away.

What were Chase's faults? Allie wondered. He'd kept them pretty well hidden so far.

Allie stood and took Trey's hand.

"What about us, Allie?" he asked.

"I'm clueless."

Trey pointed her back to the sofa and sat by her, holding both her hands and locking eyes with her. "Let me make this easy for you," he said.

Allie held her breath.

"I don't think we should marry," he said.

Allie's heart jumped.

"I'm not sure I love you," he explained. "If I did, I wouldn't have stayed so removed from this . . . whatever it is . . . this quest for your dad."

He paused, but Allie found no words to say, so he took

179

a breath and pushed on. "I'm not sure you love me either," he said.

"But I do," Allie insisted, although she wasn't sure what she meant by it.

"Not the way a woman should love the man she's about to marry," Trey argued.

Allie dropped her eyes as he said plainly what she'd recently concluded but didn't have the courage to verbalize.

"We seemed so right for each other," Trey continued. "Right age, both prime for marriage, reasonably compatible. It was so convenient for both of us. But ultimately it's wrong."

Allie squeezed his hands and looked at him, gratitude rising in her heart. "You're stronger than I am," she said. "I couldn't have broken up with you this close to the wedding."

"This is better than a divorce," he said. "Although Mother doesn't want me to marry you, she'd kill me if I did and then divorced you later."

Allie laughed, and the tension in the room relaxed. "Your mother is a pistol," she said.

Trey grinned and shook his head. "I'm all she's got," he said. "Sometimes much to my chagrin."

Allie kissed his hands. "We'll find the right person," she said. "We have to believe that."

"I think you already have," he said.

"You mean Chase?"

"Yeah."

Allie's heart warmed as she considered the possibility, but she didn't want to say anything to hurt Trey, so she shrugged it off. "I'm clueless there too."

Trey opened his mouth, but Allie put a hand over his lips. "Let it go," she said. "My fiancé just called off my wedding; it's not the time for me to worry about another man."

Trey kissed her on the forehead. "You're a special person, Allie Wilson. I hope you'll still be my friend."

She hugged him, then leaned back as Gladys walked in, a doctor beside her. "They're moving your dad," Gladys said. "Guess it's time to go."

Allie and Trey stood and walked out of the hospital with Gladys, each of them wiping away tears for all different kinds of reasons.

Allie met Chase two hours later at a restaurant in Decatur a few miles from the hospital. He stood as she walked in and pointed her to the table he'd chosen for them.

"You and your mom get things situated?" he asked.

"Called the funeral home in Harper Springs," she said as she sat down. "They'll pick Dad up in the morning; funeral is set for Saturday at eleven o'clock."

"You can still make your wedding," he said.

"Not going to be any wedding."

His mouth dropped open, and she quickly told him what had happened with Trey.

"He called it off?" Chase asked.

Allie nodded. "Said he didn't love me."

Chase raised an eyebrow. "I'm shocked," he said.

"Still a little numb myself."

A waiter arrived with two glasses of water and set them down.

"Are you okay with his decision?" Chase asked as the waiter left.

"He did what I didn't have the courage to do. I admire him for that."

Chase sipped from his water, his brow furrowed with obvious thought. "I still can't believe it," he said.

"It's true. I've made some calls already—the minister, the florist, the caterer. Trey's taking care of canceling the travel arrangements, the photographer, the limo service. Do you give back wedding presents?"

"You're asking the wrong guy."

"I think you do." Allie pondered the work ahead. "It's not as embarrassing as I thought it would be."

"You're not back in Harper Springs yet," Chase said.

"You're no help."

The waiter brought bread and butter with menus. They thanked him, and he walked off. Chase leaned forward, his elbows on the table, his hands clasped.

"Look," he started. "I told you that God wanted me to marry you, but if that had anything to do with what happened with you and Trey, I take it back; don't want that on my conscience in any form or fashion."

"No," Allie said. "What Trey did . . . it had to happen. Not your fault."

Chase wiped his brow. "Okay," he said.

Allie fixed a piece of bread and butter, handed it to Chase, then took a drink of water. Chase nibbled the bread.

"Well?" he said as he swallowed.

"Well what?"

He faced her, eyes dead ahead. "Are you going to marry me or not?"

Allie choked.

"Easy!" Chase said. "I'm not trying to scare you."

Allie wiped her mouth with a napkin and slowly caught her breath. "You're not serious?" she said.

"I don't mean tomorrow, but one of these days, once we know each other better, once you've come to love my charms, my looks, my sensitivity."

"Your humility?"

"That too."

Allie grew serious. "You really believe God wants you to marry me?"

"Do you believe God wanted you to find your dad?"

Allie hesitated, still unsure how to answer that question. "Let's just say I'm not closed to the possibility," she said. "Something brought me to him, I know that. Just don't know what to call it yet."

Chase beamed. "That's where you start," he said. "If you're open to truth, I believe God will lead you to it."

"I'm open," she said. "Seeking, in fact."

"Good," he said. "I can't marry a woman who's not a believer."

"So you're putting conditions on it?"

"No, God is."

Allie started to raise a mock protest but refrained. After all, if Chase wouldn't marry a nonbeliever but God had told him he would marry her, then that obviously meant she'd inevitably become a believer. The thought of that soothed her more than it bothered her, so she let it go.

Chase grinned widely, like he knew something nobody else did.

"What?" she asked.

"I still can't believe Trey broke up with you."

"You might call it a miracle," Allie teased.

"So I really do have a chance with you?"

Allie's grin now matched his. Although her dad had just died, her fiancé had just canceled their wedding, and the doctor had told her her father had died from complications from a genetic disease called Marfan syndrome and that she needed to receive testing for it, she felt happier than she could remember. Against all odds she'd found her dad before his death, found him in time to assure him of her forgiveness and love and to hear him express his love to her. Not only that, but a caring, handsome, intelligent man sat across the table from her—a man who had walked with her through a quest she'd never imagined starting, much less completing—and he said he wanted to marry her. In the midst of hard times, good things were still possible.

"Do I have a chance with you?" Chase asked again.

Allie took his hands in the center of the table. When she spoke, her eyes sparkled. "Let's just say I'm not closed to the possibility."

Epilogue

Saturday, Two Weeks Later

Allie and Chase climbed out of Chase's truck and hauled the last of the wedding gifts Allie had to return into the post office.

After handing them to the attendant, Allie wiped her hands and faced Chase. "Glad that's all over," she said.

"How many gifts did you give back?"

"Over two hundred. Thank goodness I didn't have to mail but thirty or so."

They hopped back into the truck and headed to Allie's apartment. She rolled down the window and enjoyed the feel of the June air blowing through. A warm late-morning sun baked down on her, but she didn't mind. The heat helped her relax, something she finally felt she could do after surviving the blur of the last few weeks.

Offering countless explanations about the cancellation of the wedding, grieving her dad's death, undergoing a series of medical tests at the Asheville hospital—each had taken its physical and emotional toll. She sighed, glad she had the whole summer without school to regroup.

Chase turned left and pointed the truck up a small mountain road.

"Wrong way," she said.

"There's a little roadside trail overlooking the valley up here," he said. "I found it last week on the way back to Knoxville. I've got a basket lunch." He nodded toward the truck bed, and she glanced back and saw a wicker basket and a cooler wedged against the side. "Thought you might enjoy a walk, then maybe a bite to eat," he said.

"You bring insect repellant?"

"I've prepared everything—a blanket for when we eat and a UT cap to cover your eyes from the sun. You relax and enjoy."

Allie knew she had one more thing to do before she could really do that. Chase drove a couple more miles, then pulled off and parked, but Allie grabbed his arm and stopped him before he jumped out.

"What?" he asked, facing her.

Allie bit her lip, a little afraid to tell him what the medical tests had revealed but absolutely certain she needed to do it. "You know those tests I told you I had to have?"

"Yes."

Allie clenched her fists. "I got some results back yesterday, and I've inherited the disorder that led to Dad's death."

Chase turned more in her direction.

"It's called Marfan syndrome," she said.

"I never heard of it."

"Few people have, but about one in every ten thousand people have some level of it; it's a disease that affects connective tissue, the glue that holds the body together. It can affect the lungs, the eyes, the skin, the spine, the heart."

"But you're healthy as a horse."

"I'm not sure I like that comparison, but you're right. I've always been healthy, played basketball, everything I ever wanted to do."

"Then what's the problem?"

"It can affect me later; that's what it did with Dad. It caused problems with his heart, his aorta."

"But he fought in a war."

"The effects often show up as a person gets older."

"How so?"

"The doctor explained it to me this way. When it affects the heart, it's usually the aorta—that's the main artery connected to the heart. In people with Marfan syndrome, the aorta isn't as flexible as usual, since connective tissue is used to build it. Since the aorta is so close to the heart, it's subjected to the full force of the heartbeat. This pounding can, over time, wear down the aorta until it ruptures."

"Did your dad's aorta rupture?"

"Not completely. If it had, he would have died in minutes. But since he was already in the hospital for problems related to his years of drinking, they found the problem before that happened. His aorta was weak though, eventually too weak for them to fix."

Chase took off his UT cap and brushed back his hair, then placed the hat back in place. "And you've got this syndrome?"

"A mild case, but yes."

Chase glanced out then back to Allie. "How serious is it?"

"Not too bad right now. With modern medications and

surgical techniques, the doctor said it's plenty manage-able—as long as the person is aware of the problem and takes corrective action as it becomes necessary."

"Anything you need to do now?"

"Make sure my blood pressure stays low. That lessens the stress on the aorta and heart valves. Don't play contact sports."

"So we'll never get to play field hockey together?"

"Strike that off your list."

Chase rubbed his eyes. "Can you still have children?" he asked.

Allie noted the implication of the question. "Yes, though a child might inherit the disease from me."

"But not necessarily."

"That's right."

"What's your life expectancy?"

"With care and treatment as necessary, pretty normal."

Silence fell between them. A bee buzzed into the truck then back out. Chase stared out toward the mountain.

"What are you thinking?" Allie asked, fearful of the si-lence, fearful that he was trying to figure a way out of their budding relationship now that he knew of her ailment.

Chase took off his cap and set it on his knee.

"What?" Allie pressed.

When he faced her and took her hands, a small tear rolled from his left eye. Allie felt certain he was about to tell her good-bye. She braced herself.

"I wondered why," he said softly. "Now I know."

"I don't understand."

"The search for your dad—this is the main reason. So you could find this out, take the precautions necessary to protect your health."

Allie squeezed his hands. "You're not going to leave me over this?"

"Did you really think I'd do that?"

"I didn't know."

He bent to her and kissed her, the first time ever. She felt his lips, smelled the woodsy smell of his cologne. She hugged him and realized she'd never felt this way about Trey, never felt this way about anybody. Safe, comfortable, completely loved.

She lingered in his arms for another few seconds, then placed her head on his shoulder. He stroked her hair. She leaned back and gazed into his eyes.

"I can't believe I'm with a UT man," she said.

"I can't believe I'm with a heathen," he teased.

"Converting you might be harder than converting me," she teased back.

"I'm counting on that."

Allie snuggled into his shoulder once more. "I think you can," she whispered. "I think you can."

Gary E. Parker is the author of nineteen published books, including *A Midnight Miracle*, *Secret Tides*, and *Fateful Journeys*. He currently serves as the senior pastor at First Baptist Church in Decatur, Georgia, and is a popular speaker on college and seminary campuses. He lives in north Atlanta.